Select praise
from Amazon readers for
RENOVATING CHRISTMAS
by

LESIA FLYNN

Painting Skyline

Skyline Mountain Book 2

LESIA FLYNN

Painting Skyline Copyright © 2014 Lesia Flynn

Cover Art by Lesia Flynn with contributions by MJTH/Shutterstock and pavels/Shutterstock

ISBN: 0990990818
ISBN-13: 978-0-9909908-1-9

For those who choose to move forward.
They are our true heroes.

ACKNOWLEDGMENTS

First, I would like to say a very special thank you to my family and friends and to my readers for your encouragement and support. I could not have done this without each of you. Thank you for believing in me and for pulling the story out of me. I truly appreciate your love.

I would also like to say a very special thank you to my chapter mates at Heart of Dixie. You ladies are the very best and I am fortunate to be in your midst. Thank you for your encouragement and support all along the way.

My heartfelt thanks goes to Elizabeth Vershowske for her patience and superb editing skills. But mostly for laughing together with me and helping Bear and Julia's story come alive on the pages.

And finally, thank you Matthew Cooper for answering all of my crazy questions about cycling. If there are any errors about the sport or its equipment, they are entirely my fault.

CHAPTER ONE

"WHAT DID I do to piss you off now, Princess?" Bear stood there dripping pool water.

Julia gawked at him. He appeared to weigh mere ounces and made of air from the way he propelled himself out of the Olympic sized pool with grace and efficiency. But he was. Well. *Ginormous.* And beautiful, if you liked the bigger-than-life-bear-like-appearance of a carefree, confident southern jock. She had a clogged pipe or something because air wasn't flowing in or out of her body.

He laughed. "I see you ignore my existence, yet again." He leaned down and grabbed a towel off the lounge chair nearest to him and began methodically drying himself without taking his eyes from her. "That's the way of it then. We'll just go on behaving as if I don't exist." He turned his back to her then and threw the towel over his shoulders before retrieving his shirt and keys. He slipped his feet into a pair of flip-flops, lifted his bike under arm, and moved toward the gate, her existence as invisible to him as she insisted he was to her.

Just as he waved a hand in the air, a salute to his final departure, Julia gathered herself enough to clear her throat. "That's not what I meant."

Bear stopped with his hand on the gate, listening.

"I mean" Julia squeaked. She adjusted the book and towel that were clutched to her chest before clearing her throat to finish. "You're not invisible."

Bear turned around with eyebrow raised, as if to ask, *did I hear you correctly*?

Her shoulders slumped. She sighed and let her head fall to the side lamenting the years of confidence training she'd worked through, but now stumbled to her feet in complete betrayal of her character.

Bear turned back around, fully facing her and closed the distance between them. He stopped close enough that she could feel the heat coming off of his body. He showed no emotion, but she could sense his intensity just the same. A muscle twitched on his jawline. His eyes softened. "What *did* you mean, Princess?"

Julia couldn't breathe. She could barely think a thought to completion what with him standing so

close and looking down at her. "I um." She looked
at his lips peeking through his overgrown beard.
"That is to say." She turned her eyes towards the
wall of the pool area that overlooked spectacular
views of the surrounding fall painted mountains. "I
don't." She shivered. It was seventy-eight degrees
with no wind whatsoever. Her hands were cold and
she shivered, again. He smelled of man and pool
and sweat and heat. His skin glistened a warm
brown proving his love of the outdoors. She looked
down and noted his toenails were clean and tidy and
white and neat. There was a white strip of skin
peeking out from underneath his sandals. A fleck of
periwinkle blue paint stuck to the "v" of his left
shoe. *He must've worn them while working*, she
thought. Julia closed her eyes and drew in a deep
breath hoping for its cleansing powers. She exhaled
slowly. When she opened her eyes and dared look
back up into the face of the man who'd hunted her
for months, she saw a smile gleaming back at her. A
smile that was wide and generous and patiently
waiting for her response.

Julia laughed at herself. "I'm sorry. I didn't
mean to offend you. I didn't mean anything at all."

"So I'm to think you were just taken in by my
god-like appearance and rendered speechless, is that
right?"

Nailed it! She thought inside her head.

3

"But of course you couldn't say that because that would indicate that you noticed me and that's just not your style, is it Princess. Being royal and all. Right?"

Julia winced. "Please don't call me that."

"But isn't that what you are? A privileged young woman who has everything she could possibly want or need. Sounds like royalty to me."

Julia once again let her head fall to her chest and looked downward desperately trying to gain control of herself and maybe the situation. She bit her lip just as a large hand lifted her chin back up towards the sky.

"If you'd stop looking away maybe we could get past this little boxing match, sugar."

Julia couldn't help but follow the movement of his lips. Just as the word "sugar" left his mouth his tongue slipped out and licked his lips leaving a trail of unwelcomed provocative thoughts skipping across her mind. And still, she couldn't look away. *So what, she'd sworn off men. She could still look. There wasn't any harm in that.*

Bear's nostrils flared just enough to pull her eyes up a notch. A tree branch jostled behind her as a squirrel leapt from one tree to another. Bear's thumb reached up and smoothed across her lips. A dove cooed in the distance to her lover.

Julia's heart fluttered.

Bear's eyes dropped to half-mast and zeroed in on her mouth. "I think you're a royal pain." He then bent, reaching for their lips to collide.

Julia heard alarm bells ringing in the back of her mind but she squelched them and let herself be led to wherever he wanted to take her. His lips touched hers, lightly at first and then all she could think was how marvelous it was that his lips tasted like honey. Golden, delicious, liquid honey. Something sounded in the distance, a horn or maybe a whistle. She paid it no mind and made a noise of her own when Bear pulled the things from her arms and threw them behind her onto a chair. He slipped his hands back down to her sides and pulled her in tight against his big body. Her pulse ran fast and hard and now she was glistening with heat where less than five minutes ago she was cold as ice. A banging sound broke through the air as a car door slammed against its frame.

Julia jumped back and gave Bear a shove. A flush of embarrassment painted itself up her neck and all over her face before she could hide behind her hands.

Bear looked at the cover of the romance book he'd tossed out of her hands and let out a low growl in recognition of what the cover promised. Passion.

Confusion swept through Julia. She'd never in her life wanted to feel such strength and desire as that which Bear was dishing out but she knew she shouldn't encourage him. He'd been in pursuit for months now, always backing down when she told him no. But her body wasn't telling him no. It was screaming yes so loud inside of her she was certain he too could hear its screams of desire.

Bear pulled his arms across his chest and rocked back on his heels. "Well. Well. Well." He winked at her then and let a dimple peek out at her. "I think we've got ourselves a royal on the run."

Panic grew and escalated inside of Julia. Once again she couldn't speak, couldn't even think fast enough to respond before an arm slipped past her and she found herself once again within the paws of a bear, his lips so close she could feel the hair on his face tickle her as his lips moved.

"What are you afraid of, Julia?" His eyes bore down into her soul requiring her to cough up an answer. "Please put me out of my misery and tell me, what are you afraid of?"

She couldn't do it. She couldn't say a thing. His mouth moved to take hers into his control and she heard herself squeak. Squeak like a damn mouse terrified of the big badass lion, or bear as it were.

"I am not running the YMCA around here, Mr. Grecco!" Dicker stood a foot away from them, hands boldly on each hip, steam coming from his ears at a rate a large earth moving shovel would envy. In customary fashion, he sported loud plaid golf shorts, a screaming orange shirt, and a whistle around his neck in true self-appointed-Skyline-Mountain-lawman style. "Who on God's green earth gave you permission to come up on our mountain and use the pool facilities any time you feel the need to do so, sir?" Dicker turned and looked accusingly at Julia then. "And you! You haven't exactly been the poster child of conformity either, little missy! What gives you the right to break the rules and share this wealth with the likes of him?"

If there was anything, or rather *anyone*, who was enough to pull Julia back to her warrior self, it was Dicker. "Let me tell you something, Mr. Dickerson."

"Now, now, now." Dicker waved a finger in rejection to her salutation. "Miss Julia, you know I request that everyone call me Dicker. Not Dick. Not Mr. Dickerson. Just Dicker. It's the right thing to do here in the south where we all behave with impeccable, friendly hospitality." His mouth spread generously across his face almost making Julia believe he was being friendly.

"Dicker! Shush! You are a bully and a faker. Stop telling me what I can and cannot do. I won't have it. I pay my mortgage and my Home Owners Association dues just like the next guy and you have no right to tell me what to do. Besides, I wasn't using the pool for crying out loud! I came up here to enjoy the sunshine and I got accosted by a Grizzly!

Bear held an offended hand over his heart. "A Grizzly?" He let out a howl of laughter to the sun that made the tree branches sway and squirrels giggle in response. "You have *got* to be kidding me!"

Julia reached over and punched Bear in the arm.

"Hey!" He smoothed a hand over the offended arm. "What was that for?"

"You!" She pointed at Bear and huffed. "And you!" She swung around and pressed a finger into Dicker's face. "Men!" She exclaimed in frustration before bending to yank up her belongings and take off for the gate.

"What the hell was that?" Bear shouted in her wake. "You're not running scared, are you?"

Julia turned back to face Bear, and with all her twenty eight years of maturity and polish, shot him the finger. Then she stiffly turned back around, carried herself regally through the gate, and put as much distance as she could between them before her knees gave completely out from underneath her.

What she didn't hear in her wake was Bear sneering at Dicker.

"You have amazing timing old man."

"Maybe you're just not moving fast enough, Mr. Grizzly. Looks to me like you need some hibernation time to work out your strategy?" Dicker slapped at his knee reveling in his own delivery of fun.

Bear growled. "Yeah, well you need to mind your own beeswax, Dicker."

Dicker pulled himself as tall as his body would stretch and aimed his finger up toward Bear's face. "Maybe so. But mark my words, Mr. Grecco. There's a bear on this mountain that needs to go swimming somewhere else. Fishing too, from what I just saw of Miss Julia punching you in the arm." And with that, Dicker spun on his heels, opened the gate and ushered Bear to the street.

LORD HAVE MERCY on her soul. Julia had never considered herself a red hot, passionate woman. And she certainly wasn't a world savvy one either, what with that unfortunate money incident with her brother. If she was that gullible with him, she was certain to be a huge target for people she didn't even know, bears included. And that presented her with the very real likelihood of remaining single for the rest of her life. Sadly, her grandmother reiterated that notion every time she saw her, claiming Julia could never trust a man with her heart because he'd run off with her "goods" before he could ever love her.

Her grandmother wasn't at all surprised that Julia had found herself lacking in the savings department after her star-child brother pulled the wool over her eyes and took off with her money. Of course, her grandmother thought he deserved it if he could pull such a thing on Julia without her notice. Granted, it wasn't a truckload of dollars, but it was enough of a start on life. That unfortunate incident had been four long years ago and several therapists in its wake. It seemed money was a lot easier to come by than rebooting her self-esteem, though. She was good enough at working hard and earning money. Not so much so in the confidence department. But she worked hard at it, harder than most. And for what? For a bear of a man to waltz right up to her and dismantle every ounce of fortitude she'd worked so hard to attain. She couldn't win for losing! First it was the money. Now it was her dignity.

None of it mattered right now though. All that was important was that she had escaped a near collision with one mighty big bear whom she was certain would maul her if given half the chance. He was a man, after all. And men liked to handle, to maul, and to paw their way around a woman. At least that's what she heard her coworkers at the school talk about in the teacher's lounge. She had to agree given her history with the few men she'd dated over the years. They tended to mess with your head, too. But not this time. She was smart. She was well on her way back to finding her own personal independence and she was not going to be distracted by a man, no matter how big and scrumptious he was.

Julia stuck the key into the lock at her tidy little house on the end of Skyline Drive just as a familiar voice rang out though the trees.

"Hi, Miss Julia!" The voice came from the direction of the street, out from among the little girl giggles of surrounding friends. It was Rudi, Jon and Christy's little girl.

Someone from the group piped up beyond the giggles, poking fun at Rudi. "You called her Miss Julia."

Rudi bounced right back, pride written all over her face. "I can call her that away from school. She's my friend, isn't that right, Miss Julia?"

Julia approached the group and pulled Rudi into her side and squeezed. "That's right, Rudi. Besides, we're neighbors, too."

"We're headed to the park!" One of the girls invited. "You want to play with us?" A little white puppy peeked out from the arms of one of the girls and joined them in the verbal exchange. The young girl set him down to jump around them in his excitement, careful to hold onto the leash.

Julia laughed at the girls and their puppy. "It looks to me like you've got a handful there." She knelt down to touch the bouncing ball of fur, unable to resist the draw of its white fluff. "Who is this little guy?" Puppy kisses greeted her as she scooped him up. Giggles chorused all around them, fueling the exuberant animal.

"This is Puff. She belongs to Traci and *she's* only two months old."

Traci shyly smiled and added, "I tried to call her Marshmallow but it was too much of a name for her. So my daddy suggested we call her Puff. You know, like a marshmallow?"

Julia smiled and reached a hand across Puff's little head as the pup wriggled her excitement. "I think Puff is a fine name for her." Julia agreed.

Puff jumped in her arms at the sound of her own name and started barking at them like she had a voice in who went to the park, her little puff-tail waving like a banner of joy.

Julia laughed. "I think she's trying to get y'all to hurry up and get to the slide!" Puff barked her agreement.

"Won't you come with us, Miss Julia?" Rudi pleaded and the others all chimed in their pleas.

Julia knew they all adored her at school from the all-too-often times they showed up in her classroom. "Thank you girls, but I've got a date with some sunshine and a book on my back porch."

The collective let their disappointment show, but seemed to understand. She was their teacher, after all.

Julia handed the puppy to one of the girls and waved them off towards the park across the way. Trees were changing colors and the air was a little cooler. Pumpkins and chrysanthemums were beginning to dot the landscape even though the temperatures were not giving up on summer just yet. Just the same, decorations were coming out and making ready for ghouls and goblins to hustle through the streets collecting treats.

Julia smiled, remembering last year's jack-o-lanterns. She had refused to throw them away after Halloween and continued to light them every night until after Thanksgiving in abject rebellion to Dicker. Of course, that's when Christy, Rudi's mom, and Jon Frazer met while putting out Christmas lights for the annual Skyline Christmas event. They had fallen in love around the traditional Christmas festivities on Skyline Mountain. Jon had proposed in full Dicker-rebellion-style with Valentines as his Christmas yard art. Come Valentine's Day there had been the most beautiful homespun wedding Julia had ever seen. Christy wore lace and Rudi gave her momma away to the one they both loved so much, Jon Frazer. Even Dicker made a fuss over them at the reception, gifting them with a lovely crystal double heart ornament for their new family Christmas traditions. Julia sighed. Yes, it was lovely the way they found each other and made a family.

Would she ever? Could she leave herself open enough to take a risk and find a love like that? Her mind calculated the likelihood of being in love. She pulled the novel she was squeezing next to her chest away and scanned the cover which illustrated unrestrained passion. Holy cannoli! She had been in a similar embrace just minutes ago. Just the reminder of it made her want to run and hide. Maybe she just wasn't cut out for such sensualities. A flash of the view to her "lingerie" drawer passed across her mind. Sure enough, her granny panties would never get her voted *Sexiest Woman Alive*, that's for sure. Julia groaned and headed to her back porch getaway. After all, one could escape reality if you set your mind to it!

A GOOD WHILE later Julia awoke to the sound of her phone buzz-buzz-buzzing on the table next to her long-ago-emptied iced tea glass. It was Christy texting her.

"Heard you had a run-in with a bear...you okay?"

Julia tapped her keys to respond. She stopped to look at her toes which were now in full view of the sun and mocking her with their bright pink glare. Crappit. She'd fallen asleep in the shade to wake up in the sun. Not good.

"I'm fine. Come have tea on my back porch?"

She never took naps in broad daylight so clearly she was bored with her own company. And it was only day one of Fall Break. She needed a rescue. Or she could break her own personal vow to relax and go inside to work on her latest crochet project for the women's bazaar at her grandmother's church.

"Sure! Be right there."

Julia laid her book face down to save her place on the chair and headed inside to freshen up her glass and pull a little something-something together for her friend. The sudden contrast of the dark in the house made her blind, but she fumbled around and gathered up a few cookies and two tall glasses of iced tea. As she put everything on a tray, she mentally tallied the projects she already had ready for the church ladies and decided not to force another item into her plans. If it happened, it happened. If not, she had plenty to contribute to help raise funds at their annual event. Satisfied with tea and cookies, she headed back to the porch to welcome her friend. That's where she found an intruder . . . of the grizzly kind.

He was sitting on the edge of the trail that lead out from her yard looking out over the little town of Riverland, Alabama below. He seemed particularly focused on something, she could see the muscles in his shoulders rippling through his shirt. But she couldn't tell exactly what he was doing. She was torn between the fact that it was *her* yard, but then it was a public trailhead, too. What to do? She didn't want him here! He made her feel things. Things like, things that made her *feel!*

She didn't have a chance to do anything because at that precise moment Christy popped through the side gate and, seeing Bear first, gave a shout out to him interrupting whatever it was he was doing.

"Oh hey, Christy." Bear stood easily in his big self and turned toward Julia. In doing so, Julia noted the camera in his hand and excused his trespassing ways. She couldn't deny the fact that even she herself had wanted to take pictures of the changing leaves out over the mountain. Apparently that was something they shared, an artist soul and all that. But when she looked back up to the man's face, there was nothing hidden in his features. He was a man on the prowl. And for the second time that day,

Julia felt a shiver run through her body in the heat of the day.

CHAPTER TWO

GIOVANI COLOMBERA GRECCO, better known as Bear to all who knew and loved him, stood watching as the woman he wanted dug in her heels, or bare feet as they were, to get rid of him as fast as she could. He didn't much mind, counted it as further challenge, in fact. Because, as God was his witness, he was going to have her if it was the last thing he did. It wasn't a vendetta or anything. He just couldn't seem to get her out of his head. He'd already spent far too much time in the wee hours of the night wondering what she wore underneath those practical pencil skirts she was so fond of. A thong or cheekies, maybe? A pushup or was that *au naturel*? And that little thing she did with her lip when she felt threatened, that one just about drove his fantasies to explosion. And this had been going on for almost a year now, since last

18

thanksgiving. He was a patient man, but this was going to stop. Today.

He rubbed his belly as if hungry for the next course and nodded his head in her direction, recognizing the move only infuriated her more. His face split wide in a grin that could only say, I accept the challenge and raise you one, *sugar*.

She didn't offer him any tea and cookies, he noted. It made him smile. She was a live one, Julia. And he liked it. Yes, today was going to be the day the action changed around here. And he was the one who was going to roar in delight at the end of the day.

"Do you *ever* work?" Contempt laced the words Julia slung out at Bear.

He barked with laughter. "Only when I have to, sweetheart. Only when I have to. Besides, you know the old saying, *love the work you work and work the love you love,* or some such thing.

Julia rolled her eyes at him. "No, its *Work is not work if you love what you do.* Confucius said it."

He picked up her glass and took a long draw on it letting her watch his throat as he swallowed the sweet nectar. He could see Julia all but groaned out loud at the sight of him.

Christy cleared her throat and raised an eyebrow at Julia, letting out a laugh to soften the inquiry. "I think you both have it wrong. Wasn't it Dr. Seuss?"

Bear threw his head back and laughed.

Julia's forehead scrunched up so tight you could hear the wrinkles gathering for communion. "I'm sure it was. Really!" Christy nodded as she popped one side of a vanilla sandwich cookie into her mouth. "He said . . . *When he worked, he really worked. But when he played, he really played.*" And with that last 'played', she wiggled her eyebrows suggestively at Julia.

Bear howled even louder as he pulled Christy in to his side. "My comrade!" He bent his head down to kiss the top of her head.

Julia threw up her hands and turned, throwing herself into a chair to pout.

"Oh don't get your panties in a twist, Julia. We're just having some fun." Christy plopped down next to her and removed the two sides of another cookie to lick the cream.

Bear leaned against a post, leveling his eyes on Julia once again, devouring her. Without a move, he directed his thoughts at Christy. "Are you and Jon going to that benefit bash that's coming up soon?"

Julia squirmed. Clearly she was having a hard time containing whatever it was she was feeling. Maybe, for all the smoke she was huffing and puffing, her body was humming the tune he wanted to hear her sing.

"I don't know. We want to, but I don't have anyone to watch Rudi. You know how she is. Even if she was old enough to leave her home alone she'd likely have the entire neighborhood enthralled in some new project of hers."

Julia perked up her ears. "What benefit? And why don't you see if Rudi can spend the night with her friend Tracie?"

Bear cocked his head to the side. Curious. Now what would a benefit do to spark such interest from his woman?

Christy reached for another cookie, this one chocolate, and pulled her knees up to her chest in the chair wiggling her toes over the seat's edge. "I guess I could. I just hate asking people to take her. I'm a weirdo about that, I know. It's just not my thing."

Julia reached a hand over to Christy. "I understand, really I do. But I'm thinking she has one friend in her group whose mother would be relieved to have Rudi stay overnight with her girl."

"Yeah? Who's that?" Christy scraped the icing with her teeth.

"Tracie, you know, the little girl who has the puppy?" Julia gave Christy time to nod. "Well, her daddy just went back on another tour of duty. I'm sure it's been quiet around their house with him gone and extra work on her mom, too."

Christy stilled and thought about it. "I didn't realize." She knew firsthand the trials of mothering while her man was over fighting for others' rights. She'd lost Rudi's daddy years before when he had served to help others. It had been a long time before she could even let Rudi out of her sight or anyone else into their lives.

"Please think about it before you decide not to go."

She had compassion where it mattered, Bear thought. Noted.

"So tell me, what's this benefit all about?" She looked him in the eye now, all business ears.

"It's a fundraiser my sister put together for the new Children's Center for the Arts in Riverland. They're building an interactive art center as well as a gallery of some sort. Anyway, they're auctioning off some artwork to raise money for the facility." Bear reached overhead and pulled the band from his long hair. He ran a hand through the thick waves gathering it back again, and reformed it into a neater ponytail.

"Oh they're not just auctioning off artwork. They have an original *Giocco* up for bid to bring in the masses." Christy reached for the plate of cookies again.

"Why do you think it'll bring in the masses?" Julia questioned.

"Anonymity, I suppose. He's flown under the radar not letting anyone in the art world know who he really is. He's all *mysterious*. Until now, that is. They say he's going to personally attend this event, which he's never done before. And he's announced that he plans to go public with his identity, which rumor has it, celebrities are lining up to attend out of curiosity." Christy temporarily turned her attention back to the cookie she held. Twist. Turn. Lick. "I heard Riverland's own Rina Pearl is taking a break for one night from her tour to attend." Christy set her cookie aside, wiggled her eyebrows again. "I wonder if *Giocco's* one of those stuck up artist types who values himself more than he should."

Concern skittered across Bear's face briefly before he cleared his throat. "Anyway, its black tie, dinner, auction. And an open bar and dancing all night after." Bear smiled. He let his eyes narrow in on his target. He breathed through his nostrils.

Julia's breath caught on an intake of air.

"Be my date, Julia."

It wasn't a question. It was a command. And it visibly rattled Julia.

Christy didn't give Julia time to catch on before she piped up. She dropped her feet to the ground and scooted to the front of her seat. "Oh yes! Let's go together, shall we? And make it a double date!" She clutched the edge of her seat to anchor her

23

excitement. "Julia we can go shopping and get new dresses and have our hair done! It'll be a grown up night of fun! Right?" She questioned Bear.

Bear grinned his approval of her team playing maneuver.

"Say yes, Julia! Please say yes?" Christy pleaded with her eyes.

Bear returned a powerful hold on Julia with his own pair of eyes. "This should be right up your ally, being royal and all." He couldn't help himself. And damned if he hadn't just doubled the bait.

And right there, all of a sudden like, Bear snagged his woman with the help of his sidekick Christy. And Julia hadn't even seen the bait before she stepped in and got herself trapped by the bear.

FEELING ENCOURAGED BY the outcome of his photo-hike, Bear parked his old truck under the gnarled oak tree in the back alleyway. He unloaded his bike from the bed of the truck, shouldered his camera, and entered his studio. After leaning the bike against the time worn brick wall, and hanging the camera from a protruding hook left from old meat scales, Bear prepared to work.

It was his favorite place in the world, this old building. For as long as he could remember his father had used it as a market to sell meats and specialty items only found in his homeland, Italy. But as the tides of life flow in and out, Bear's father had gone to sleep and left the old building wanting for another era of work. It only seemed right for Bear to use it for his own business. He had so many memories here, happy memories, pictures of love and life, warmth and care that his father had shared freely with him and his five sisters their whole lives.

So with the help of his mother and sisters, he'd cleared everything out. The coolers, the shelves, the baskets and racks. The only remnant left of the old world of his father was the worn sign painted on the outer wall of the building that faced the street, speaking of a simpler time go by. Now all that the old room housed were the paints and brushes of his trade. Photos hung by clips across a wire between two walls. Orders and receipts stacked neatly in a bin near the front display window that he'd sealed with black canvas to keep onlookers from discovering him. And stacked all about the space were more canvases of every size imaginable, more than he cared to count. It was work. It was his dream. His life.

An old swivel piano stool that had long ago been separated from its musical mate stood in front of an easel. A blank canvas invited him to sit and replace the white of its surface with color and emotion. Bear sat, but his mind went to another work and he turned to face it. A large canvas leaned against the wall, filled with landscape and light, but lacking in the emotion he was so well known for. He'd started that painting not long after his father's death but had since searched for what to fill it with. It was a nice landscape, but it was flat. It was devoid of something he couldn't put his finger on. But he knew it would come to him. He just wasn't sure when. Or what it would be. But it *would* be. Someday.

He sighed and relinquished himself to the work at hand. He had recently accepted a commission from a school mate from the University of Bologna where he'd spent many long hours painting and discovering his talents while living with his mother's sister and her family. Outside the city they had a farm, to which Bear had ridden his bike to and from on a regular basis. On many a rainy day over the course of his college years, his cousins had rescued him and his bike from the weather. He could still hear his aunt fussing about him riding *che parafulmini* in the thunder and rain. Bear smiled. His mother often said the same thing on this side of the ocean, *that lightning rod.*

As he worked the canvas and brought hue and tone to life, Bear thought about Julia and wondered what her childhood had been like. Had it been full of love like his? Full of family? He didn't know much about her other than the undeniable fact that he wanted to know everything about her. He wanted to learn her background, her dreams, and her aspirations. He wanted to find what made her laugh and smile and lose control. But more and more, he wanted to discover who she was behind closed doors, beyond the inhibitions and veils she was so adept at hanging between them. Who was the real Julia Thurston and how could he pull her out of hiding? And with that, he buried himself in work, batting one idea around after another to figure out how to win his woman's heart.

CHAPTER THREE

IF IT HADN'T been for the fact that Julia had been following the recent growth of one famed artist named *Giocco* she would have backed out of the benefit date-decree, even with the potential of mingling with the parents of her school children. Many of them would undoubtedly attend the event. It would be the perfect opportunity to entice them into cooperation for her school projects on the horizon. But *Giocco* was taking the art world by a storm and frankly, she was as curious as the rest of the world. Sure, sure. He was probably a great maestro of the paintbrush, but his business anonymity was what intrigued her. No one knew exactly who he was, just that he gave all of his profits away to one charity or another, rarely (so the story goes) keeping anything for himself. There was rumor he took excellent care of his parents, but no one seemed to know who they were either. His works were starting to litter the southern states about as plentiful as kudzu. Thankfully for the charities he favored, the price of his works were continuing to rise. And for the art collectors out there, it was a sure investment. At least that's what the art community was saying.

So Julia was willing to eat her pride (and maybe her hormones) for one night with a bear for the opportunity to mingle with locals and celebrities alike. Perhaps, if all went well, she could feast her very own eyes on the up and coming *Giocco*. But that wasn't going to make the next few weeks pass any easier. Somehow she knew, since a bear was already in the house, he had every intention of playing. Every chance he got.

So Tuesday morning when her phone rang as she was pulling out her hooks and yarn to start a Christmas blanket to give to someone in need at the local nursing home, she wasn't a bit surprised to hear Christy on the other end.

"Come go to lunch with me and Rudi, please? We're taking her friend Tracie and her mother Donna to *The Tea Room* and then I thought maybe you and I could do a little shopping while we're in town if we can get Donna to bring the girls back up the mountain for the afternoon."

And that is how Julia came to find herself standing in front of *Angelica's* looking at a little black dress she wished she had the figure and complexion for. Its curves hugged all the right places, conservative yet insinuating at the same time. It dripped with elegance and richness. She wanted to feel the fabric slip through her fingers and wondered how it would make her feel to move inside its finery.

Christy laughed. "Come on! That dress is calling your name." She took Julia by the hand and pulled her into the store where a lovely dark haired fairy like young woman escorted them to the dressing rooms with organdy and silk flying behind her in waves.

But that one dress in the window called her. It knew her intimate parts. And when she put it on, even the little fairy woman sighed. A tuck here, a pin there and *Voila!* Looking back at her in the mirror was the most delicate and beautiful masterpiece of softness and elegance she'd ever imagined. Everything about her melted and turned to butter. *Was that really her? Julia Thurston?*

"Well, that's settled. You are the only woman anyone will see at the Benefit." Christy laughed.

"Wait. Is this for the *Benefit for The Children's Center for the Arts*?" The saleslady's eyes ate up her entire face in their questioning drama.

"Why yes!" Christy exclaimed. "Julia and I are going. We can't wait. It's not often Jon and I have a chance to go on a date without my daughter."

"You don't mean Jon Frazer, do you?" The fairy questioned.

Christy showed a slight concern.

"Oh it's okay. It's a small town, remember? Jon Frazer is my brother Bear's oldest and dearest friend. So you must be the new Mrs. Jon Frazer. Christy, right?"

Christy let her defenses rest. "Yes. I'm Christy. I'm sorry I didn't mean to be alarmed."

"Oh don't think anything of it. These days you can't be too safe, I suppose." She smiled and turned to Julia. "So you must be Bear's date for the evening?"

Julia felt her face flush. This was his sister, after all. Lordy but for a hole to swallow her up right now. Ick! Family always made her itch in discomfort. She reached her neck to scratch knowing full well it was already flaming red and betraying her.

The fairy wrapped a hand around Julia's arm in comfort. "He's all bark, I promise." She rolled her eyes. "And I know he seems a mess, but he won't be that night."

The fairy woman's eyes danced in mischief making Julia wonder.

"Besides, he wouldn't dare do anything to cross a sister. And he has five of us, you know. Five Italian divas to keep him in line."

Julia nervously pulled on an ear that threatened to make her scratch like a hound. "So can you promise me he won't be wearing flip-flops and bike shorts to the event?"

"I'm sorry", the petit woman extended her hand to Julia. "I'm Angel, his third oldest sister." She shook hands firmly, offering an encouragement. "I assure you, he will be in best form for the evening."

"Interesting. And why is that?" Julia chanced a glance in Christy's direction who was entertained by the whole business of Bear as the topic of choice.

"Oh, he'll be in excellent form because his five sisters will have nothing less than the best in attendance at their side." She nodded at Julia.

Exiting *Angelica's* with an armful of packages that promised of glam and fun, Julia stopped in front of a window two doors down that showcased a large painting, an Italian landscape. Behind it, the rest of the building was blocked by black canvas draping the back of the display window. "I've never noticed this shop here before, have you?" Oil paintings, dotted the floor under the feet of the large easel showcasing the landscape. A wire dropped from the ceiling empty of a previous display.

Christy turned to face the window alongside of Julia. "This building has been here as long as I can remember." She looked up and pointed to the old fading painted sign that simply read *Market*. There was a standard office supply "Closed" sign hanging in the door. Its window was backed by black canvas as well. Darkness and quiet hung behind the windows all but for the sunshine reflecting on the pieces in the showcase area.

Julia noted a signature at the bottom of one of the paintings with an unusual crown emblem next to it. *Giocco*. Huh. "Look Christy." She pointed at the signature. "It seems like *Giocco* might already be in town."

Just then the door over *Angelica's* jingled as Angel joined them on the sidewalk. "I wouldn't get attached to that painting in the window if I were you. It's not going to be there after the Benefit."

"Is this the one they're auctioning off?" Julia asked.

"No. I don't think so. It's just that when there's an auction, all of his other works sell like hotcakes." Angel winked at them. "He's really good, don't you think?" She smiled broadly, enjoying the Tuscan landscape in the window.

"Wait. Do you know him?" Christy asked.

Julia leaned back and looked at the building again. "Sure! You must know him. You work right next to each other."

Angel popped her keys into her shoulder bag and pulled out a pair of stunning Gucci sunglasses and slid them over her big beautiful eyes. A smile filled her fairy face. "Sure. I know him." She slid her glasses back down to the end of her nose so they could see her expression. "But don't tell him I said he's any good. It all goes straight to his head and I don't care to inject him with any more junk than he's already got." She laughed out loud then, sending trills of mischief through the air as she skipped away. "*Ciao*, ladies!"

Julia looked at Christy. "That was odd."

Christy laughed and turned to walk down the sidewalk where they'd left her car.

Julia chased after her. "Don't you think that was odd, the way she *knew* him?"

Christy pointed her keys and clicked the door locks. "Sure, I think it's strange." She rolled her eyes at Julia and wiggled her hands in exaggeration. "Oooh! A mystery *artiste* with an ego! Sure, strange that one. Nothing like aliens landing on Skyline Mountain kind of strange, but. . ." She let the idea trail off as she climbed into the car.

Julia looked back at the building. "I bet there's a story there, *Giocco* and Angel!" She hopped into the car beside Christy and nodded. "There's a story there. I just *know* it!"

About that time a bike whizzed past them on the street.

"Hey look! There goes Bear!" Christy exclaimed.

"Speak of a man with an ego. Geesh!" Julia looked to heaven and shook her head in bewilderment.

THE SUN SET heavy that night as storms threatened to bring cooler weather behind it. The smells of autumn danced on the breeze. Julia sat on her porch watching as the clouds roiled in their varieties of grey. Thin shreds of pink trailed in the distance and the last of the sun fell below the horizon. She balanced a glass of red wine on the arm of her chair as she lounged back and reflected on the day. It had been one of the greats in the big scheme of things. For the first time since moving to the mountain, she felt a true bond with someone, Christy. It was nice, that feeling of connection. After that ugly situation with her brother she'd been afraid to let anyone too close and as time ticked by there simply wasn't opportunity with anyone until now. Therapists were hardly friends. Christy had a way of making her feel like family. Important. Needed. Valued. Most importantly, she didn't take a thing from Julia except her presence and friendship.

What a welcomed change to not be suspicious or guarded. To have a friend.

"Any chance I could get a glass of what you have?" Bear carried his bike over a shoulder as he approached.

Julia bolted out of the chair, spilling red down the front of her white shirt. "Crappit!" She uselessly wiped at the stains left. "Why do you do that?" Exasperated by her inefficiency of cleaning up the mess, she set the wineglass down with a little too much force and followed up with slamming her hands on her hips, letting her face say exactly what she was feeling.

In true form, Bear rubbed his middle and let out a howl of laughter, his beard waving mockery right back at her. Tattoo ink peaked out from under his watch band enticingly. Julia followed the movement of his hand with her eyes. It shouldn't be so seductive dancing around the muscles, luring her in. Her brow wrinkled in response. Her girl parts cooed inside and she recognized her inner woman saying something about wanting to climb the man like a tree. She mumbled some nonsense out loud, telling her woman to shush, all the more making Bear laugh harder.

"You!" She pointed at him. "You don't belong here." She pointed her fists to the ground. "My house!" She stomped a foot. "Go. Away."

Bear let his laughter blow away into the breeze and eased up to her cautiously like she was a momma bear in protection mode. He slipped a hand easily around her waist. "You. Sit." He cajoled. "I'll make everything all right." He pushed her gently back to her seat, picked up her glass and disappeared behind the screen door.

Julia was spitting mad. The very idea of him taking over her, her, her *porch*! This was her porch! She stood up and marched into the house growling, gearing up to take him down.

Bear turned just as she entered the kitchen and handed her a new glass of wine, tipping it with his own in the process. "To you, sugar."

Julia deflated. *To me? Wait, what?* She watched him as confusion played across her own features.

Bear sipped.

Again she watched as the simple movement of the man taking a drink made her insides go to mush. She spun on her heels and marched back outside where it was safe, taking a full throttle slug from her glass.

"You might want to slow down there, sweetheart." The screen door made a bumping sound as Bear followed close behind. "I don't want to have to carry you off to bed or anything."

"If anybody's carrying me anywhere, I assure you, it won't be you!" Out of spite she took another long drink, giving him a sidelong glance as she did so. Fear gripped her mind.

Bear grinned and shook his head, making his beard shift in ridiculous fashion.

"Don't you ever shave?" *That's it. Push back*, she thought.

Bear grunted. "If there's the need."

"Why don't you shave every day? You should shave every day. Better yet. You should go to work every day, too. You don't do that either, do you?" She was getting smug with herself as the heat of the wine soothed her nerves and her insecurities drove her. "That's why you drive that beater truck isn't it. You don't want to work so you don't have a decent truck."

Bear went quiet. Listened. Let her take her shots at him.

"Your momma must be *so* proud." *Lordy but she was proud of herself about now, all southern polish forgotten.* She had the bad manners to actually sneer at him.

He nodded. "She is. Tells me so every day, in fact." He leaned over and set his glass down, gently. Bear measured the distance between them with each word he spoke. "In fact, Julia. She says she wouldn't want me any other way than what I am today." By the time he spoke 'today', Julia's eyes were seared to his lips which were now directly in front of her. Denial pumped through her mind as her body screamed its desire. Bear watched the war play out on her face.

"Are you going to kiss me?" She asked, still watching his mouth.

"That depends." His lips taunted her dancing behind all that hair.

Julia reached a hand up and ran it through the curls hanging from his face. She expected it to be wiry and harsh, scouring, in fact. But to her sensual delight, the man's beard was soft, making her want to dive in and languish in all it had to offer. It was like cotton candy. It was soft and she wanted to bury her face in it. She inadvertently slipped a finger across his lips.

"You're playing with fire, Princess. Careful you don't ask for something you don't really want."

Julia's' eyes shot up at him then. She pushed at his chest. She gasped in horror at herself. "What do you want from me?"

Bear leaned back where she could watch his eyes, dark with hunger. His breath eased in slowly, measured. "I want all of you, Julia. Every single ounce of you." He let her go then and turned around to face the storms heading their way.

Julia stumbled at being unhanded. She was flabbergasted. She held her chest where her heart hid, pounding out a cry of disappointment she was certain could be heard at the base of the mountain.

"Storm's almost here." He took a sip of his drink. "I guess I should be going so I don't get caught in it." He reached beyond her and set his glass next to hers. When he pulled up to height, he took her hand into his own and ran a finger across it admiringly. "You're a delicate woman, Julia." Then he leaned down and kissed her gently on the knuckles. When he stood back up, he locked eyes with her and simply held her there. A flash of light fingered its way across the night sky. Thunder crashed in the distance. "I don't take what's not mine. But I'm about out of patience here. Whatever you're afraid of, deal with it. I'll be back." He turned, shouldered his bike and walked toward the side of the house.

Julia came to her senses and shook her fist in his wake. "I'm not afraid of you, you big bad bear!"

Bear gave his customary wave over the head.

"I'm not!" she insisted. Right before she fell off the three inch porch slab.

CHAPTER FOUR

BEAR BROODED OVER a cold one at Jon and Christy's, rubbing at the gold band label around the bottle's neck. He'd known the bottom was about to fall out of the sky. Riding a piece of metal down the mountain was borrowing trouble he wasn't willing to pay for. Besides, Christy had a pie coming out of the oven any minute and he didn't want to miss that particular yum.

Christy turned off the water at the sink, dried her hands and folded the towel before turning towards him. "Are you going to spill it or am I going to have to pull it out of you?" She quirked an eyebrow at him. "I can't help you out anymore if you don't tell me what's going on?"

Rudi swung into the room giggling, took one look at Bear, apologized, and ran in the other direction as Jon held the door behind her for her escape.

Jon slid into a chair at the table and aimed a finger at Bear. "Stop scaring my girls."

Bear growled.

Jon hooted with laughter.

"Yeah. You laugh now. I remember a few months back you not being so happy about being turned away yourself, traitor."

"Hey! I was never turned away." Jon pulled Christy's hand and tugged her down to sit on his lap, drawing her in tight. She laid her head against his shoulder. "You never turned me away once, did you beautiful?"

Christy smiled as she burrowed her eyes into his. "Not once." She touched her nose to Jon's and laughed. "Well, there was that little sidestepping action I did after we saw Dicker's lights that night. But I didn't turn you away. I just hid out for a day or two." She dropped her lips to his before shoving off to turn the oven timer off.

"Harrumph. Sidestepping." Bear grumbled and leaned back in his chair before closing his eyes.

Jon glared at Bear. "I *know* your momma didn't let you lean back in *her* chairs." Jon eyed Bear, daring him to challenge. "Sit up *boy*! That's my new floor you're putting dents in." He commanded.

Bear set his chair back down to the floor. "New floor my. . ."

"Watch it. Wife. Daughter. Choose your words wisely, my man."

Bear ran a hand through his beard and nodded at the floor. "Looks nice, by the way. Bolton came through for you this time."

Jon grinned wide. "Yes he did. Came through so well I've got enough to lay down in the garage apartment, too."

Bear nodded. "I'm glad he's pulling himself together." The room went quiet. The sound of music wandered in from the front of the house in its wake. Bear fidgeted and slumped down in his chair, relaxed, "What do y'all know about Julia? I mean *really* know?"

Jon and Christy looked at each other and simultaneously lifted their shoulders in the universal I-don't-know move like they had practiced it their whole lives together.

Christy handed Bear a plate of apple pie with vanilla ice cream already melting around the edges. "I know she's a good woman and she works hard."

"That's not what I mean." Bear filled his mouth and rolled his eyes toward heaven, pointing his fork in Christy's direction then nodded his complete approval toward Jon. Talking around his full mouth he mouthed, "If you ever stop loving her, I call dibs."

"Mine." Jon ground out forcefully around his own full mouth.

43

Christy laughed at the both of them and settled herself against the counter, crossing her arms in thought.

"So what's got your interest peaked, Bear?"

He pulled his plate up close to his chest, pushed his long legs out in front of him, and crossed them at the ankles before digging in for another forkful. "I don't know. I get the idea she's afraid of me. No. Not me. She's afraid of people in general." He filled his mouth again, let his appreciation rumble in his chest, and retreated in thought.

"Well, I don't know anything about her personally except she stood up to Dicker's ridiculous Christmas light rules by leaving her jack-o-lanterns out until Thanksgiving. So, she's got grit in her somewhere."

"Does anyone really know where she's from? I mean, did she come from around here or move here? And why does she live all alone, isolated?"

Jon and Christy exchanged a look and shook their heads.

Rudi peeked around the edge of the swing door. "Momma?" She eyed Bear with trepidation. "Can I have some pie?"

Jon laughed and pulled her into the room and let her lean into the safety of his side. "You can't have any" he provoked. "It's all mine!"

"Don't you dare let him get away with that nonsense, sweetie." Christy handed her a plate, licking the cream off her fingers as she did so.

Rudi held her plate steady, watching the thick white liquid run down around the sides of the pie. "Are y'all talking about Miss Julia?"

Bear cocked his head in her direction.

"We were just wondering where she's from is all" Christy said. "Bear likes her and we were trying to figure out how to help him get to know her better."

"She likes puppies!" Rudi grinned.

Christy and Jon laughed simultaneously. "Do you know anything else she likes, baby?"

Rudi wrinkled up her nose. "Not really. I just know she's pretty wonderful. All the kids at school love her." She licked her fork. "Booger Hayes says she goes to his church sometimes with her grandma."

"Yeah?" Christy eyed Bear, effectively nailing him to his chair in silence. "Who's her grandma, do you know, sweetie?" Christy waited.

Jon soothed a hand over Rudi's back as she ate and thought.

"It's some old meddling woman in town." She scrunched up her face, turned her head as she tried to remember. "Something like Thurman or Thornton or some such?" She raised her eyebrows in delight of the next bite of pie. "I don't know. Somebody grouchy is all I remember."

Jon, Christy and Bear groaned in unison, "Mrs. Thurston." Everyone knew Mrs. Thurston. She was Riverland's version of Dicker and up in everybody's business.

Bear slid his plate and fork to the table. "I should've put the two together a long time ago, she and Julia." Being careful not to tip the chair backwards, Bear leaned his weight back into the chair. He ran a hand over his beard, thinking. "I've always known Mrs. Thurston had family. She and Julia are just so different, night and day really." He hung his head in thought and finally made a sound as if accepting his own conclusion. "Being Mrs. Thurston's granddaughter certainly explains why Julia's always on edge. I'd be on edge too if that woman was my grandmother."

Jon agreed. "Mrs. Thurston's an intimidating force, that's for sure."

Bear grunted. "That woman scares me."

Rudi's eyes got big and round. "I didn't think bears were scared of *anything*!"

BEAR ENTERED THE old house the way he always did, through the back door. He stopped long enough to wipe the storm off his feet and rearrange his ponytail, slipping a hand over his beard when he was done just to make sure he wasn't dripping.

"Anybody home?" He called out into the darkness. *Power must be out*, he thought, as he moved through the kitchen. He figured it would be. But even more certain, he knew his mother would be worried putting bedtime off until the storms passed.

Just as he rounded the fridge, a petite woman slipped through the hallway door with a candle in hand. "Oh! Son! I'm so glad you're here." She sputtered a laugh at herself. "I was a little spooked by this terrible storm we're having." She reached up and hugged his neck, careful to hold the flame away from their bodies. "But you shouldn't be out in this *weather*!" Again, she laughed before her facial features took a turn to mama-drama. "You did *not* ride that bike of yours out in this mess, did you?" A hand flew to her hip. She waited.

Bear took the candle from her and set it in the center of the stovetop. "No, Mama. I dropped my bike off at home when Jon drove me down the mountain. Then I hopped in my truck to come over and check on the first love of my life." He bent and laid a kiss on the top of her head.

Paola Raimondo Grecco, or Mama Paula as everyone around Riverland and the surrounding area knew her, was the queen bee in this Italian family. She might be small in stature, but she was a mighty force to reckon with if you crossed her babies. Especially if you messed with her only baby boy. It didn't matter much that he was a grown man. He would always be her baby boy.

"Son, that truck. How do you *drive* that thing?" she tsk-tsked.

"Just like you drive yours, Mama. Put the key in. Turn the ignition. Put her in drive."

Mama Paula slapped at him playfully. "Don't you get smart with me, son." She laughed.

"I take it your power's out?"

"Yes." She sighed. "It's been out now for about an hour. I expect the power company will get to us as they can."

"I bet Mrs. Thurston called it in the second it happened."

Mama Paula groaned. "Don't you know it, son." She shook her head. "That one will never change. I suppose we should be grateful she's on top of things, but. . ."

Bear eased over to the kitchen table and sat. "Actually, she's why I'm here. In a manner of speaking."

"Oh?" Worry crossed Mama Paula's face. "Why is that, son?"

"Well, now, before I get into all that. . ." Bear had the good sense to look sheepishly at his mother knowing full well it would reel her in, "you wouldn't happen to have anything to eat in that fancy fridge of yours that'll go bad before the electricity is back on, would you?" He let his face split into high-beam straight at her mamma-bear heart.

"Oh you know I do, son!"

Bear laughed out loud at her, so predictable, his mama.

Mama Paula got busy pulling out this and that from her refrigerator. She was always prepared with food. It was her Italian way, love by way of food. He had no idea how she did it or why she bothered since she had lived alone now for several years. But her cupboards were always full of *delizioso*!

Mama Paula put a 'nice salad' in front of him and ordered him to spill while she put together a plate of antipasto.

"So. There's this girl. Woman, I mean."

Mama Paula stopped what she was doing and did a little dance in her kitchen, reaching her hands to heavens and giving thanks to the Lord above. She mouthed something in incomprehensible Italian to the Mighty One directly.

Bear groaned. "Now, don't go getting yourself excited. You haven't heard what I have to say yet."

She pulled herself together all serious like and shook her spoon in his direction. "Right. Yes sir. No excitement." The smile left on her face could not be contained. She shook her spoon again. "So spill, already. I'm getting old just waiting on you! Ha!"

Bear shook his head at her. "Old my ass." He smiled at her, letting his love flow. His mother was the greatest in the land, loved like no other and would always be his first true love. More than that, she got him. She comprehended all his gears and mechanisms. And she encouraged him at every turn.

Bear made short of his woman story, filling her in on the few things he knew and maybe retaining the better part of his interest in the woman to himself.

"So that's it."

Mama Paula placed a plate of olives, salami, and cheese in front of him. "If the power comes on after you've finished that, I'll warm you up some lasagna," she said. She pulled a bottle of wine and two glasses from the buffet and slipped into a chair across from him.

"I was wondering if you knew of a granddaughter of Mrs. Thurston's. And if so, do you know anything about her?" He reached for the glass of wine she poured and drank.

"Hmm. I don't know son. You know I don't spend time with her if I don't have to. She makes me feel bad things, that one."

Bear laughed. "Bad things, is it?"

"I don't know. I'm sure she has her value. She just makes me feel judged. Less. Like she's more and all that."

Bear reached over and took her hand in his big paw. "Then I don't ever want to hear of you spending time with her." He squeezed. "Nobody is better than you, Mama. Nobody."

Mama Paula ran a hand over her heart. "Oh son. I wasn't fishing for adoration."

"I know that."

She smiled her pride at him. "But it means the world to me that you think so. I love you, son."

"Okay. Stop that. Drink!" Bear clinked his glass to hers. "To Mama-drama love!"

She let out a hoot. "To Mama-drama love it is!" and she drank before leaning back in thought. "You know, I could ask around a bit."

Bear growled. "I just told you no socializing with the woman."

"Or you could use some of that money you've got hold up and pay an investigator." She grinned, letting a little bit of manipulation edge her words. "That's what your Papa would have done. Paid somebody to do his dirty work."

Bear rolled his laughing eyes at her. "Papa didn't *have* any dirty work! He was a butcher, for crying out loud."

"Da! *Mama mia*! He could've been in the *Mafioso*!" She hitched her shoulders at him. "What?" She laughed. "It could've happened! We're Italian, after all!"

"You're too much, you know that?" They laughed amiably. "You should've written crime books, or directed film noir. You've got a knack for it."

"Ha! When did I ever have time to write a thing? I was too busy writing life with my children and with your Papa."

The lights flickered throughout the house. Bear looked up. "And let there be light." He tipped his glass in her honor. "Thank you, Mrs. Thurston!"

"You want me to heat you up some of my lovely lasagna?" She wiggled her eyes at him.

Bear thought about his night. First he had a sip of wine. Then a beer. He followed that up with pie and ice cream. Now this. Salad, antipasto, more wine, and lasagna. "Sure mama. Warm me up some lasagna and then I'll head on home and hibernate till the morning."

"That's my boy." She squeezed his arm. "And then you'll catch that young woman of yours and give me some grandbabies, right?" And laughter trailed.

CHAPTER FIVE

THE STORMS PASSED and left a breath of
early winter in their wake. Julia pouted. She'd
wanted to try reading her book poolside again today
for a last go at getting some sun on her legs before
winter set in. Of course, she knew like everyone
else that rain was sure to come with the cool down
of autumn. Still, she stuck her bottom lip out like a
two year old. She wasn't handling this self-
declared-no-work-holiday very well. She checked
the weather. Great. More rain was predicted for
later in the afternoon, lasting through the midnight
hours with a low temperature threatening frost.

What to do? What to do? She picked up her
coffee cup and began to wander her small house.
The living room was neat as a pin. Sofa, tables,
lamps. The blanket her grandmother had given her
was neatly draped over the reading chair. Not a

speck of dust in sight. She walked across the entryway to the dining room. Table, chairs, china cabinet. All stood ready to entertain. Again, no dust anywhere. Looking through the window, she noted a tree limb on the ground. Bradford Pear leaves clung to the window's screen, too, both evidence of the storms of the night. She thought about cleaning up the limb and any other debris only to look down and have her pink and white bunny slippers smile back at her, each with two toes peeking through the end of the shoes as if her bunnies had bucked teeth. She wiggled her toes and wandered down the hallway toward the first of three bedrooms. Upon entering the room she set her cup down on the bedside table and walked to the window. Again she could see the tree limb laying in the yard. She considered the tree. *Too bad it wasn't a big sprawling Oak. A tree swing would be lovely*, she thought. She sighed, slumped, and hugged herself. Dropping the idea of the swing, she turned and looked at the bed. *This would be a cozy little girl's room looking out over the park.* Not wanting to follow that train of thought since she didn't even have a mate, she moved to the closet, opened the door and looked to find two boxes neatly stacked on the shelf and five empty hangers awaiting her next visitor. The floor laid bare save for the luggage rack leaning against the back wall. She closed the door and leaned back against it in defeat. *What am I going to do with myself? I don't know how to do anything but work.* Maybe her grandmother was right. She was useless.

She retrieved her coffee, took a sip and moved on to the next room. This was the room she affectionately called The Green Room. Oh it wasn't green in color, but it was *au naturel*. Everything in its interior was a product of nature. She had an entire wall of textiles. Fabrics were folded and housed neatly on the lower shelves of the wall. A diagonal system above was filled to overflowing with color categorized yarns of every type; cotton, wool, silk. Next to a hand carved Lion Chair she'd found on a day trip to eastern Tennessee lay a basket of wool to sculpt into marvelous shapes. An oak valet stood across the room draped with a mantle of morning glories and daisies, floral scarves she'd made from the most beautifully colored wools. Hanging on the wall opposite her storage wall were her wisdom words, words she lived by or at least tried to live up to if she could. She looked back over her favorite room. Her room of solace and all things wonderful. Her place of refuge. Still, nothing out of place.

Across the hall was the only bathroom in the house. She made a habit to always leave it as good as or better than she found it so there was no use going inside to check its interior.

Last she wandered to her bedroom, the master suite. Upon entering the space, to the left was a seating area. There she had painstakingly hung curtains and placed two overstuffed reading chairs, a table, and a lamp to enjoy the view. In the center of the room was her bed, as yet unmade. *Finally something to do.* But she walked past it and beyond into what was possibly a nursery at one time. She had turned it into a garden room with all its open windows looking out over the mountainside. The view was still on the grey side of the spectrum rain wise. But when the sun returned the trees would glisten their seasonal array of spectacular color and life. She pinched a withered leaf off of a pot of ivy and examined other plants in the room before looking back out over the mountain. If it weren't raining, and a guarantee of failure, she'd slip on her hiking boots and follow the trail to the bottom of the mountain. That was asking for trouble on a day like today. But she did wonder where it lead to. Not for the first time the question of a bear's den inhabiting the side of the mountain popped into her brain.

As if conjuring up the beast by her thoughts, a man emerged from the back corner of the lot and came in full view of the window. Bear looked straight at her through the window panes. His hands were full of tree limbs, his hair hung loosely around his shoulders dripping rivulets of rain, and his shirt clung to him like a second skin.

Julia sucked in a breath and unconsciously covered her heart with one hand.

Bear grinned wickedly.

Righteous indignation enveloped Julia and she searched hopefully for a curtain to yank closed between them only to find the room she loved most with windows wide open. She huffed. She puffed. She turned and stormed away from the eyes of Bear and heard his laughter through the windows mocking her in the blowing winds.

She kicked the bunnies, ripped at her pajamas and was dressed with hair brushed and lips glossed in less than a minute. She grabbed her keys and purse, leaving her bed unmade and marched headstrong for the door that lead to her car. Which was exactly where she found Bear, leaning on the front hood, patiently waiting.

Julia ground her teeth and groaned angrily as yet again she stomped a foot.

"Now, I don't know where or who you came from, sugar, but that's no way to greet someone around here." He pushed his big body away from her car and stepped between her body and her getaway. "In fact, if I was a more sensitive man, I might just take that as an insult." He reached his hands for her.

Julia screeched as she backed out of his reach. "Don't even think about it, buddy!"

"What?" Bear tilted his head to the side, teasing her. "It's not like I was playing in the mud back there." He stepped toward her again, taunting her, playing with her.

Julia put the car between them. "Don't you dare put your paws on me Bear. . . Bear. . . Bear?" Her face crinkled in thought. "What *is* your last name, anyway?" Her hand lifted the door handle quietly but before she could pull it open he was there behind her, pinning her against the car door without even touching her.

"The real question here is this, Princess."

He moved his mouth so close to her ear she could feel the heat coming off of it as he breathed. "What's that?" She squeaked.

"The real question is," he drew out slowly, utilizing the southern drawl to his advantage, "what are you running from, Princess?"

He touched the end of his nose against the top of her ear so lightly she thought she imagined it. Julia looked at his hands splayed widely across the roof of the car in front of her. No evidence of mud or dirt to be seen. His hands were clean. And big. And tanned. And beautiful.

He pulled a hand back and gently eased her hair to the side giving him access to her neck. His lips touched her there and she all but melted to the ground for the seduction that he was.

Bear growled next to her ear. "There's nothing to run from." He nipped at her skin and slipped a hand around her waist still keeping distance between them with his body.

Julia let her head fall back into him.

He took her other hand into his and returned it to the roof of the car, held under captivity of his own. "You're safe with me, Princess. It's okay to let go and be with me." He pulled her back against him then, letting her feel the heat exuding from his body into hers. His right hand slipped just under her blouse to softness of her skin and teased just before he spun her to face him, taking both hands into his own and holding her captive.

Julia's breathing defied her. Quick short breaths escaped her. "What do you want from me?" she panted out watching as his eyes closed half way and he licked his lips.

"I already told you once." Bear moved in close to her mouth and whispered to remind her. "I want all of you Julia. Every last ounce of you."

Only the single word of "W*hy*?" escaped her as he took over her lips and devoured them right there against the car in the open garage for all the world to see, pressing his big bear self against her, enflaming her inner woman to kick into life in response.

He smelled of rain and power and man. He felt like strength and earth and certainty. He looked wild eyed as he pulled back long enough to gauge her desire. She heard a sound escape him just before he delved in to taste her deeper, letting her feel all the man he was against her. And he tasted of passion and life and freedom like she'd never known existed.

The harsh sound of metal clanging against metal broke them apart. "What the devil is going on around here, Missy? Don't you check your yard after a storm for damage?" Dicker stomped right up to the two of them and looked up into Julia's face and pointed his authoritative fist toward the street. "You've got broken limbs out there, girly. Get on it or the rules will take you down for it, I guarantee!" He let his eyes nail her to the floor before turning to march off. "And lands sakes alive! Take your cootchy-coo business somewhere else! We've got young impressionable children around here!" His head shook in disapproval as he carried forward to harass the other neighbors.

Bear growled. "I don't like that man" His head rested gently on Julia's forehead as he cupped her head between his big hands and ran a finger over her swollen lips. He reached lower and kissed her softly. "Every time I see you I want more of you, Julia. I've told you twice now. I want all of you."

Julia swallowed, engulfed in a war of fear and hope.

"You think about that while I go pick up your storm debris." He pulled her to see him eye to eye. "But know this, Princess. If you run away, I'll come after you."

Oh in her mind she wanted to scream for him to promise he would find her. She wanted it more than the next pull of air into her lungs. She looked at his lips and sucked air instead. It was all she could do with heat billowing off of him in waves aimed at her. And then she nodded her agreement.

Bear backed away from her, still holding her caged in by his big arms stretched out against the car. "Drop the keys, sugar."

Shaken in disbelief, Julia turned her head, questioning him.

"You heard me. Drop the keys." His eyes were dark and hungry. He wasn't going to look away.

Julia dropped the keys and all of her girl parts went on point.

Bear kicked the keys toward the street. "Good girl." He drew in a deep breath before letting his eyes fall to her lips. And then he took her into his mouth quickly and left his mark by way of sucking a "pop" sound on her lips and moved away from her.

She was stunned. A fog wrapped tightly around her brain in an unrelenting hold as she watched him walk away, prancing for her eyes only. He looked so satisfied at having the upper hand by the way he

stretched his glorious body in front of her. *Show off.*
But he was majestic. Powerful. Demanding. Cocky,
even. Yet, patient and kind. She couldn't deny that.
Something inside her moved and fluttered awake. A
leap, maybe. And she leaned her head back against
the metal of the car and did as he suggested. She let
herself enjoy the show of the man and watched, as
he cleared her yard, his eyes searching her out at
every turn. She should run, and run hard. But she
couldn't remember how to make her legs move.

BEAR PACED HIMSELF, not wanting her to
watch him run all the debris to the curb and right
back to her in less than sixty seconds. So he
watched her, taunted her really. And he cleared
branches and broken limbs as a show of his muscle
counting off the seconds until he could pull her
against him once and for all. He let his eyes find her
again. She looked drugged. Good. That's just how
he wanted her. He tossed the last of the pieces into
the pile he'd built and began his approach. They
both knew what was about to happen. That she was
still there told him she was in agreement. But
somehow his mother's voice rang loud and clear
inside his head and broke through the sensual trance

of Julia on his mind. "Son, when you meet the right girl, you'll know. Then you'll have the strength to prove your love to her. And you'll convince her that you are on her side." He stopped in his tracks and let the words take deeper root. She'd told him that when he was seventeen years old and about to go out on his first date. He'd hated those words that night. A seventeen year old boy didn't want love. He wanted to get laid. He'd hated those words every night since then. So why would they come to the surface of his mind today? He stopped and stood still ten feet away from the woman who made him growl for wanting. He watched her and let her see him patiently wait. Would she let herself run to him or allow awareness and fears to encroach and run away from him, again?

A car horn beeped. "Bear! Get in!"

Alarm washed across Julia's face as she straightened to see beyond Bear.

Bear turned to face his friend.

"Angel called. It's your Mom."

Bear stood nailed to the ground. *His mom. Angel called. What the hell?*

Julia gave him a push. "Go."

He looked at her, stunned.

"Go Bear. It's your mom!"

He nodded. Shaken, he took off running for Jon's truck.

"Let's go, man!" Jon shouted from the cab.

Bear watched for Julia as they sped away, wondering if she'd run or if she'd stay.

"MAMA DRAMA."

"What did you say?" Jon laughed at his old friend. "Say the word, my man, and we're out of here."

Bear's sisters, all five of them, the Italian Divas as he called them, fluttered around Mama Paula like she was on her deathbed. There wasn't a scratch on mama's body. Bear threw up his hands and walked out of the room. A gurney passed by, pushed by someone in scrubs headed beyond a set of double doors.

"You wouldn't make a very good doctor, you know that?" Jon said right on his heels.

"I hate hospitals." Bear growled. "Where the hell is this idiot that rear-ended my mother's brand new car, huh?" He rounded the corner and slammed right into the man he never wanted to see, Dicker.

"Watch where you're going!" Dicker blared out at the younger man.

Bear backed up a step, hands in the air, palms out. "Whoa. Just heading around the corner old man. Move aside so I can find the idiot responsible for my being here in the first place."

"You move aside. I'm looking for the same thing!" Dicker was spitting mad and proud to show it.

"Do you ever cooperate with others, old man?" Bear shook his head and looked to Jon. "What the hell?"

Jon's head was bowed, his shoulders shaking as he pinched the bridge of his nose. He turned around as if that could hide his humored disposition.

"Great. Now you're laughing at me."

Jon let it out audibly then, laughter that bounced around the concrete walls eliciting a few glares from the staff. "You'd laugh too if you saw the whole picture."

Dicker moved on past Jon checking nameplates as he paused by each door. Jon waved a thumb in his direction for Bear to see.

"Aw, hell no." He threw up his hands in defeat. "Tell me it isn't so, Jon!"

Jon cackled again as realization came together for his friend and Dicker marched right through Mama Paula's hospital door.

By the time Bear entered the room Dicker was in full blown explosion.

"What in tarnation were you thinking, woman?" His hands flew to his hips demonstrating his disappointment in her. "Stopping your car so suddenly like that? Didn't it occur to you that there might be someone directly behind you? For such a beautiful woman as yourself, you're certainly incapable of driving that vehicle of yours safely around this town."

Mama Paula sneered at Dicker ready to take him down a few notches.

Bear growled audibly and looked up for patience to be granted. He could not understand how a man could compliment and insult a woman within one sentence, but Dicker had done just that. And to *his* Mama Paula.

Bear didn't wait for patience to arrive. He picked Dicker up by the collar of his shirt and escorted him out of the room. Giggles and demands of restitution alike followed in their wake. Once in the hallway, Bear set Dicker down, retained his hold on the man, and let him have his due. "Old man. I've had enough of your meddlesome, demanding, accusing bullying to last me for the rest of my life. I have been kind enough to stay out of your way up on that mountain you think is yours. But now you're on my turf. You are not going to inflict your drama on my Mama. You got that?" Bear's eyes bore down on Dicker. "You rear-ended the car I just bought her causing not only the inconvenience of repairs, but years knocked off of my life worrying about her while Jon drove me here. *You* are at fault, buddy. Not my mama. Damages and hospital bills are on you."

Dicker sputtered his disbelief at Bear.

Bear picked him back up for good measure to make his point stick, letting the man's feet dangle in the wind.

"Set me down, young man." Dicker kicked at Bear. "I demand it."

"You say please. No. Make that *pretty please*, and I'll think about it. Until then you're hanging in the air, man." Bear dropped his head to the side, realization dawning on his mind. "Hold up. Now that I think of it, this is your second offense of the day." He turned his eyes back to Dicker and grinned a slow satisfactory smile. And then he started walking.

Comprehension of danger dawned on Dicker's face.

Bear dropped him down onto a hook on the wall. His collar held him up. His feet hung three inches off the ground. "There. Hang there and pipe down until I say you can get down. I'm going to check on my women."

"Women?" Dicker looked at Jon, face reddening by the second. "He has more than one?"

Jon howled with laughter as he ambled back through the hospital doors to collect his friend from the clutches of *his women*.

CHAPTER SIX

"GRANDMOTHER, I DON'T need nor will I take any handouts. I'm doing just fine." Julia rolled her eyes as Mrs. Thurston slipped a folded check into her granddaughter's hand.

"I'll feel better knowing you can pay your bills." She said, looking down her nose at Julia, the disappointment of the family.

Julia groaned inside. Why had she thought it was a good day to drop in on her grandmother? There was *never* a good time to see her. All the tea and cake the woman served was never enough to cover for the hurt she followed it up with. "I have a job, for crying out loud! I make more money than my bills are."

"No doubt you make a living, but I'm sure you have no room for frivolities, dear."

"Frivolities?" Julia followed her grandmother with the tray of dishes as she worked her way to the back of the post WWII pier-and-beam house. "What frivolities, *pray tell*, do you think I need, Grandmother?"

"Oh, I'm sure you'd like to go to the movies now and again." She rounded the corner of the kitchen and turned to take the tray from Julia. "Perhaps you'd like to purchase some lingerie beyond those horrid white bargain panties, I'm sure you wear." Again the accusing glare struck her full force.

Julia was mortified. Not only was this her least favorite relative, it was her *only* relative within driving distance. She was required by her own morals to keep up a relationship, minimum as it were. But this was beyond her patience. Her face grew red, confirming Mrs. Thurston's assessment of her undergarments. "It's not that I can't afford anything else. It's a practicality. I don't exactly have someone to entertain down there!" *Oh my God had she just said that to her grandmother*? She sputtered angry embarrassment. "Not that I would entertain anyone there" she paddled hard, heavier by the second, "or even could entertain someone there. . ." Where was the proverbial rock.....*please God*!

"Alright dear, don't blow an artery. Even mature women like myself enjoy the niceties of life.

Undergarments are pleasant. They make one feel feminine." She sneered. "Perhaps if you would pay more attention to your lingerie you could find a man that would put up with your inabilities."

Fifteen, sixteen, seventeen. Eight . . . how much longer would it take to reach the door and make a run for safety? "Grandmother, here is your check. Thank you for considering my need for undergarments, but I assure you I can handle this on my own." She pressed the check into Mrs. Thurston's hand. "I'm leaving now. Going home. I'll see you again in a week or so." *...after I've forgotten about this entire incident!* She amended inside her head.

"Oh dear. Don't go away angry. You know I only have your best interest in mind."

"I'm not angry, Grandmother. I'm *mortified*!" She pulled the door open and hurried down the back steps.

"Well do find a young man soon. One that doesn't have a penchant for frequent sex."

Julia rounded the back of the house and ran for her car, certain her grandmother would follow. She started the engine and took off, not slowing until she put three blocks between them at which point she stopped the car, put it into park and laid her forehead to the steering wheel to recover. Ack! But she'd just held a discussion with her grandmother (THE Mrs. Thurston of Riverland, Alabama!) about the notion of entertaining a man with her body parts! *Would that woman ever stop pushing her buttons?*

BY THE TIME Bear got back to Julia's she was gone. Her house was locked up tight and her carport was empty. Of course, Dicker drove by slowly and shook his fist through the window at Bear. Bear simply folded his arms across his broad chest and stood his ground, urging the man to drive on.

With Julia away to parts unknown, Bear had no choice but to take the trailhead down the mountainside to his own house. Jon had dropped him off to head to the next county over to bid on a new job. And of course his cell phone was right where he'd left it that morning, on his nightstand, which was why Jon had been bothered by *the divas* to come and find him in the first place.

The rain had leveled off to a sprinkle leaving the light shows behind them in the early morning hours. So the next place Bear was found was on the back of his bike riding off the stress of the morning's events. He didn't trust himself on the open highway alone today, unwilling to be on point for unaware drivers, so he made his way up and down, in and out of the quaint little town of Riverland winding his way through the neighborhoods that made up the grid around the town square. It was the same route he'd ridden as a paperboy when he was a kid. He still knew most of the folks who lived in the rows, though some had passed on in recent years. Lord knew Mrs. Thurston still clung to life, though. He hated turning the corner of Elm Street, halfway expecting her to be standing on the sidewalk waiting for him as she did her paper so many times in the past. To his surprise it wasn't her standing with her finger pointed at him, but a familiar car parked in her driveway. No investigator needed. Julia's car sat as evidence right in front of him. Mrs. Thurston was indeed someone Julia was acquainted with. Whether she was family or not was still to be uncovered.

Bear slowed to a stop and leaned his bike against an old oak that pushed up the sidewalk in front of Mr. Joe's house to the east of Mrs. Thurston's property. Mr. Joe waved from the porch. "Looky what the cat drug in!" he exclaimed as he pushed himself out of the old porch swing. "Looks like you finally found a bike big enough for those long legs of yours, son." He smiled broadly and stuck his hands in his pockets, rocking back on his heels in pride. Then one step in front of the other, he slowly approached Bear and offered up a weathered hand to shake. "How's life treating you Bear?"

Bear accepted the elder's hand and wrapped him up in a hug, slapping lightly on the old man's back the way men so often do. "It's been good Mr. Joe. Good enough, anyways. I can't complain." He smiled and released his hold on the man. "You're looking good yourself." He wiggled his eyebrows at Mr. Joe. "You must have a new girl in tow." They laughed amiably and Mr. Joe aimed his head towards Mrs. Thurston's and mumbled something about a meddling woman he couldn't seem to get his hands on. "It's good to see she's got family left that'll speak to her though." He pointed in the direction of a late model beige sedan Bear was very familiar with. "Seems even the roughest of us all needs family time and again."

Bear nodded. "You know anything about her family?"

"Well now, stories, mostly." He jerked his head in the direction of the car again. "Heard that one lost everything she had to that scoundrel of a brother of hers. Story goes, he stole her blind." Mr. Joe shook his head and sighed. "He was the golden boy everyone loved. A good boy too, once. But then after the accident he just broke. Changed his colors, if you know what I mean."

Bear didn't quite know what he meant, but he had a few pieces to work with now. "Any idea where he is now?"

"Well son, they say he ran off to Mexico or some such place. But don't quote me on it." He lifted his eyebrows and shoulders in unison. "I'm just an old man that don't know nothing." He slipped his hands back into his pockets and resumed his usual unruffled stance.

"Huh. I hadn't heard any of that." Bear ran a hand through his hair, repositioning the band. "I guess I need to stay more in touch." He smiled at Mr. Joe and shook his hand once again before returning to his bike. No need to knock on the door now. Mr. Joe had thrown it wide open for him to see.

Bear set out at an even pace thinking, mulling over the information as he rounded each and every corner of his old route. By the time he made it through the round and back to the square he had worked it all out in his own mind. He pulled up to *Old Henry's Bar B and Cue* and set his bike to rest while he ambled inside to rehydrate.

Just as he took his first pull from a bottle of water, a familiar voice greeted him from the door and before he could pull his long body up to full height, Bolton Matthews wrapped him in a neck hold and pretended to take down the bear.

"How's it going, my man?" Bolton slid onto a barstool, slapped Bear on the back and hailed Henry for a menu.

"Good enough." Bear smiled as he turned towards his childhood friend. "Didn't think I was going to make it through a scuffle with Jon the other day over that new floor you hooked him up with."

"Ah. So he got it all put in, did he?" Bolton nodded his approval. "I knew he'd love that old wood."

"Well, you should go see it now that it's in. And while you're there, wrestle a piece of pie out his new wife."

Bolton laughed at the thought. "I guess he's all domesticated now what with the little woman and a kid, aye?"

Bear nodded. "It looks good on him though. Christy's a good woman, good for him, too. And Jon seems to be made for being a dad."

"I never would've thought he would get married after being a loner for so long."

"Yeah. I guess he was saving himself all those years!" They both laughed good-naturedly over their friend's good fortune.

"Say, you looking for any work these days? Taking any bids, that is?" Bolton asked.

"Here and there, I guess. I'm considering a mural request from the elementary school up on the mountain. Did a quick one room job for Jon this past week. Why? What are you thinking?" He swiveled his barstool around to face Bolton and drank.

"I just was curious. You know I get inquiries all the time."

Bear nodded. "Yeah, painting's been good to me for a while now. I've gotten picky about what jobs I take on."

"You going to that big shindig your sister's putting on for the Children's Center?" Bolton leaned on the bar and waited for Bear's answer.

Bear turned away from his comrade and considered his response. Questions were sure to come, questions he wasn't ready to take on."

"I ask because I heard you have a date."

Bear whipped around to face him. "Word gets around fast."

Bolton's eyes danced. "Heard it's someone you can't seem to get your hands on." The laughter escaped him then, poking innocent fun at Bear.

Bear took it in stride. "Jerkface. My hands are landing just fine." He grumped, took the last pull of his drink and waved off to Henry as he slapped a bill down on the counter.

"Ooh. You're an angry Bear!" Bolton threw out with laughter.

"Call me if you've got any bids you want to pass my way." And Bear stormed out looking for the woman he wanted to put his hands on.

CHAPTER SEVEN

WITH HER HEAD laying on the steering wheel, Julia groaned out loud. Her grandmother would never get her, never support her either. They were simply from two different molds. She leaned her head back to the headrest and sighed her grief at the ceiling of her car, waiting for her face to stop burning. An abrupt knock sounded on her window and she just about jumped out of her skin. Of course the man who wanted to entertain her sensitive parts was on the other side of the window, looking like the badass man her body defiantly wanted to entertain. Her inner woman stood up and saluted the man while Julia's heart pounded out a dangerous beat. She was exhausted from the berating of emotions. She fell back against her seat. Giving in, she pushed the button on the door to roll the car window down.

"Hey there, Princess." He had the audacity to smile at her before letting his eyes drop to her lips and lick his own at their sight.

"Did my grandmother hire you?"

Bear tilted his head in question and played dumb. "Who's your grandmother? And why would she hire me?"

"Oh don't pretend you don't know. I saw you in front of Mr. Joe's talking. I'm sure you know exactly who my grandmother is and why I live on the mountain now. You were doing reconnaissance, weren't you." It wasn't a question. She knew Mr. Joe and all the other surrounding neighbors well enough to know they talked and that she was the center of the gossip mill these days after coming back to the area to stay. Most of them, her grandmother included, liked to remind her of what a good boy her brother was. Thankfully most didn't know what he'd been able to do to her. But still. It rankled her nerves.

Bear pulled his helmet off, closed the clasp and removed himself from the bike. "Pop the trunk."

She glared at him.

He lifted an eyebrow in response.

"Fine." She ground out before hitting the trunk button.

Bear easily removed the front wheel of his bike before gently loading its frame into the back of Julia's car. She watched him carry the front wheel around to the passenger side, open the door and fold himself into the seat.

Bear showed consideration for her emotions, sitting quietly on his side of the car, minding his own thoughts, as she drove to her safe place on the mountain. When she parked the car neatly inside the portico that extended out from the side of her house, she turned to him, still cloaked in raw emotions. "What now? Want to come in and pick up where Grandmother left off?"

Bear reached for her hand and wrapped it up in his own. "No. But I'd like to come in. Pour you something to drink? Let you decompress?" He slipped a thumb over her knuckles, watching for her eyes to soften. "I'm big. You can lean on me."

Julia exhaled and briefly smiled at the picture that flashed through her mind of curling up in the lap of a big fuzzy bear. Some of the frustration of the past hours escaped as she looked up into his face. "I'd like that." She looked down and watched his big hand soothe her smaller one. "I'd like that very much."

Following orders, Julia planted herself on the back porch. As promised, Bear handed her a drink then settled himself on the porch floor across from her. He leaned his big body against the support post. He didn't say anything. He just sat there watching her sip her drink.

Julia looked out over the mountain and breathed in the cool, damp air. The rain seemed to have left the world all glistening in its shades of orange, browns, and gold. She settled in her chair a little deeper, leaned her had back to rest and closed her eyes.

"What are you thinking about?"

Julia breathed in deep again and opened her eyes to look at him. "Hmm?" She reached for her glass and toyed with its rim before responding, trying to find the right words to express her mind. "Sometimes I wish I could wash away the past like the rain washes the earth and make it new again." She sighed. "It's like the rain gives the world a unique possibility of regeneration. A clean canvas." She laughed humorlessly at herself. "You probably think I'm ridiculous saying such a thing." She questioned him with her eyes. "I mean, I'm sure Mr. Joe told you my past or at least the summation of it."

"What do you think the summation of it is?"

Julia didn't expect him to ask what she thought. It startled her that he didn't judge her the way others were so quick to do. "That I'm a fool." She looked down into her glass, swirled it and watched the liquid roll around inside. "A gullible fool."

"Now why would I think you're a fool?" Bear eased out into the space between them gently, softly.

"Oh you know. I loved my brother, thought he hung the moon, even. Most of all, I trusted him and mistakenly thought he loved and adored me the same way. Only he lied to me. He kept himself secret from me. He had my complete trust and then he stole all of my money and ran off with my heart." She frowned. "To hear Grandmother tell it, I wasn't capable of keeping any savings, anyway." Again a self-deprecating laugh. "Even though my parents left it for me, I should have known he would ultimately get it. He was always the one everyone loved the most." She shook her head. "I could never wrap my head around why they left the money to me to begin with. It didn't make any sense." Julia looked to Bear as if he could explain. "Just like everyone else, they always favored him, too. Why did they leave him out of their will?" She stood then, set her glass on the table, and walked to the far side of the porch. She leaned into the column and wrapped her arms around it, watching as the sun slipped away from the high point in the sky and move towards its routine decent. "I guess I've never been very good at reading people or summing them up. I tend to trust their words rather than their behavior right in front of me. Or the other way around. Either way, I get it all jumbled up into some romantic notion of what I think people should be instead of what they really are." She rested her head against the post and sighed. "He's my brother. I thought he would grow up and be everything I thought he could be, you know?"

A hand slipped across her lower back. "It seems to me your parents thought that, too. And he should have." Bear slipped around the post and stepped down into the grass to face her eye to eye. He lifted his hand and pushed a strand of hair away from her face that the wind insisted on pushing around. "What do you read of me, Julia?"

"I don't know?" She watched his eyes, questioned him; questioned herself.

"Tell me what you see, Julia." His voice dipped low, commanding her to respond. "What's right in front of you in full view?"

She slowly shook her head. "I just told you I'm not good at this." She moved to step away and Bear pulled her back.

"Just tell me what you see. Look at me and say what comes to mind is all."

Julia chewed on her bottom lip, nervous, reluctant, pained.

Bear kept his eyes on her and gave her time to think, to respond.

"I'm not sure." She paused, looking over his face, examining his expression.

His hands rested on her hips, a thumb played soft circles against the tender skin of her sides. "Look at me, Princess. Just say the words you think."

Julia looked back into the deep pools of his eyes. "I guess I see someone who's passionate. You're certainly relentless. You're loyal to your friends, to yourself, even. But. . ." She let the word stop her.

"But?" Bear's hands stilled and loosened their hold on her.

"You're so care free." Her face scrunched up into worry. "It makes you seem unreliable, undependable. It's like you don't take life seriously."

"And how do you know that?" Bear let her go then and raised his arms clasping his hands around his neck, stretching back as he did so. "What exactly do you know about me?"

Julia shivered at the loss of his warmth against her. "I don't know anything, I suppose."

Bear reached out between them and moved his hand from side to side in the air, as if erasing the conversation. "Let's back up. Just tell me what you know. The concrete things. What do you know?"

Julia stepped down into the grass and walked over to a flowerbed, bent and picked a bud left from summer. "I know you ride a bike. You know how to swim. You paint houses for a living. You have sisters and friends." She paused and lifted the flower to her nose, inhaling as she did so. She turned to face him again. "I know that somehow you know my grandmother's neighbor Mr. Joe. You have no fixed schedule. You own a camera. And a wreck of a truck. In fact, I'd say you spent more money on your bike than your truck." She reached out with the flower and teased his face. "You don't seem terribly interested in the way you look, what with the beard and ponytail and flip flops." She tilted her head, checking her thoughts for other details hidden from the surface. "And you're not afraid of Dicker." She bit her lip then, waited for more to come to mind and when it seemed there was nothing else, she walked past him back towards the safety of her chair.

Bear let her pass before pulling her back around into himself. "You've taken notes, Julia."

His eyes were so close she could see the flecks of gold dancing with the blues and greens as a storm hovered around their edges. She couldn't breathe for the air he ate up around her. And as sure as the thunder had rumbled through the south that morning, she knew he was about to electrify her soul.

His eyes dipped down. "You know things you're not saying, Julia. Important things." His lips skimmed the surface of hers, taunting her to open to him. "But you don't know everything, it's true." He looked back at her then, letting their eyes calibrate. And then he breathed in and descended upon her mouth, devouring like a tornado touches down from the sky, ripping apart every boundary she had so carefully built.

She dropped the stem from her hand and wound her hands behind his neck, deep into his hair.

Bear growled his frustration. He lifted her into his arms and carried her through the back door of the house, searching. "Which way to the bedroom?"

Julia navigated him down the long hallway to the back of the house. At his sight of the unmade bed she apologized "I never forget to make the bed, I promise."

Bear grinned wickedly at her. "As far as I'm concerned, you just made it easier for me to crawl into it with you. All that matters to me is that it's underneath us."

Julia squealed as he dropped her onto the pillow-top softness. And then her thoughts assaulted her and she panicked, scrambling to the other side to get away. *Oh God! He's going to see my grannie panties.*

"And don't even go there, woman. I don't give a rat's ass about your panties."

"But . . . "

Bear held out his hand for her to come back to him. Julia hesitated trying to shelve the fear that insisted on beating in the forefront of her mind. "I'm not very good at this."

"At what, exactly?"

"I'm not good at exposing myself." She looked out the window. "Especially not in broad daylight." She wrapped her arms around herself, hugging tightly, still hiding. She turned back in his direction but didn't dare look him in the face. "I'm no good at intimacy." *There. It was out there in the open,* she thought. Let him do with it what he wanted.

Bear stepped around the foot of the bed and held his hand out to her again, this time taking it into his hold and pulling her against his chest. "You'll do just fine if you'll stop thinking so much, Princess."

Julia looked at him then, gauged his words, his efforts. Finally convinced, she nodded ever so slightly. And Bear began mapping her body, not leaving an inch untouched.

THE SKY OUTSIDE the bedroom window was dark when Bear woke up. Julia was nestled in tight against his ribs, right where he wanted her to be. He thought about how she had given herself over to him all afternoon long, letting him teach her how sensual she was; how intimate she could be. She had just needed the right man for the job is all.

He smiled and reached to take her hand into
his. They were so different, he and Julia. There was
the obvious, sure. He was big, she wasn't. He was
relaxed, she was uptight. But they were the same
too. They were good people. Kind. Honest. And
they fit each other. He wondered, not for the first
time, what it would be like to know each night
when he fell asleep that she would be beside him
when he awoke the next morning. Could they raise
a family with love the way his Papa and Mama
Paula had so masterfully done? Could they grow old
together and be the rock each other needed in good
times and in bad?

In thinking about his golden years, Bear's
thoughts rounded a curve and aimed themselves to
Dicker and Mr. Joe. One man so cantankerous he
likely couldn't stand his own company. But he must
be lonely not having anyone to share life with. Of
course, that would be an angel of a woman to put up
with his bad manners. But still. And the other man,
Mr. Joe, kind beyond his years and pining for a
woman he couldn't bring himself to fight to have
front and center in his life. Mrs. Thurston. To
anyone's eye, Mrs. Thurston and Dicker seemed a
more likely pair. But if together, they would kill
each other, no doubt. Perhaps someday Mr. Joe
would step out and have the guts to walk across the
yard that separated him and Mrs. Thurston and

eliminate that gap. Bear hoped so. Mr. Joe deserved his dreams like any man.

Bear rolled over and pulled Julia with him. She turned and buried her face under his arm without waking. He'd worn her out. Male pride wrapped itself around his heart. *His woman was satiated.*

His woman. He had always been territorial about her. From day one, even. It didn't make any sense, it just was. She was his woman. He played with her hair, letting it run through his big hands. It was soft and fell like strands of silk through his fingers. Again the thought of a family came to mind. A little girl with hair as soft as her mama's and a boy running and chasing life as fast as his little legs would go. His mind saw it all just as it could be. And laced through its laughter and joy was the beauty of his woman tying it all together in a package of home.

Bear's hands stilled. That was it. Julia. Home. Family. That was what the flat empty painting that stood on the wall of his studio had been waiting for. His family. Bear breathed in deeply and let the idea take root. And as he drifted back to sleep he dreamed of laughter and children and the most beautiful princess in the world.

CHAPTER EIGHT

JULIA SAT IN the floor of the green room, her lap covered in her latest crochet project. She had awakened like clockwork at five am and not knowing how to behave with a bear in her bed, she scooted out quietly, grabbed her robe and bunny slippers and tiptoed to the kitchen for coffee. Now with her cup on the table next to her and a crochet hook in hand, she let the enormity of the night's events wrap around her heart. She may not know all about the man, but she knew one thing for certain. He was her lover. At least for right now, anyways. And he was a kind and generous and voracious lover. Remembering the things he'd done to her in the wee hours of the night made her blush even to herself. And when he'd tucked her safely into his side and ordered her to sleep, something in her heart sighed and let her relax, maybe for the first time in her entire adult life. He made her feel things, lots of things. Adorable and wonderful things. But most of all he made her feel safe. She sighed and felt her heart do a little dance.

"You're thinking too much again."

Julia looked up to see Bear lounging in the doorway wearing only his bike shorts. She smiled at him. Her cheeks burned.

He cocked an eyebrow at her. "Am I going to have to take you for another round to quiet your thoughts?" His face split wide in a devilish grin and he wiggled his eyebrows.

Julia laid her wares aside, stood, and slipped into him, reaching up and running her hands through his loose hair. "I don't know that you have to, but if you want to, you can try." She let her hand slip down his jaw and tugged playfully on his beard. "Or I can get you a cup of coffee and let you think about it." She reached up and let her lips touch his, giving him opportunity to decide.

He pulled a taste from her and lingered in her softness, then moaned between them. "You taste like morning and woman and sex all rolled up in one."

Julia smiled at his assessment.

He nipped at her bottom lip.

"I take it you like mornings?"

Bear nipped again before pulling back far enough to look into her eyes. "I like you, woman."

90

His brow pressed together. "No. That's not it. I like us. Together."

Julia nodded and bowed her head, pressing it against his chest. She ran a hand down his left arm and pulled back to hold his hand in her own while she traced the lines of his tattoo. It was unusual, yet beautiful in its simplicity. Dark lines melded together to form a crown on the inside of his wrist. "Why did you get a tattoo?"

Bear shrugged. "It's just another form of paint. Why do you hide from me?"

Julia lifted a shoulder shyly. "I'm not sure what I'm supposed to do, I guess." She snuck a look upward, quickly, then let her eyes return to the ink on his wrist.

"You don't trust yourself." It wasn't a question but an assessment. "And you're afraid of me."

"I suppose so."

Bear reached under her chin and lifted her face to his. "Even after all we shared last night, you're afraid?"

Julia searched his face. Everything about him was real and bigger than life to her. Even his emotions seemed big. She ran a finger down the slope of his nose, admiring its beauty. "I don't trust my own feelings."

Bear turned and backed her against the door, holding her attention as he did so. His eyes nailed her in place. He watched her, seemed to take her measure, and then dove into her with unrelenting passion. He held her firm and devoured her with his mouth until she was panting and reaching for more. Quickly, he pulled away. "What does that make you feel, Julia?" Heat radiated off of him. His arms were cords of steel as he held her in place against the hard surface. "Do you feel alive? Wanted? Hungry? Beautiful?"

Julia was stunned into silence. All she could do was nod. And then the words followed quietly. "Yes. You make me feel all of those things." She pleaded with him with her eyes and he stepped back into her, kissing her again with tenderness and warmth as he wrapped her arms around his neck.

"You make me feel all of that and more, Julia. Every time I see you, I want you." He kissed along the line of her cheek as he moved whispering his words in her ear. "Every damn time."

Julia melted in his arms again and Bear pulled her hips into his own and let her feel the effect she had on his body. A moan escaped as her body spoke past her inhibitions.

Bear eased away from her slowly and allowed time for her to adjust to their separation. When she looked at him and the fog of passion let her see him, he spoke to her.

"I'm convinced I will always want more of you, Julia. What does your body and mind say to that, Princess? How do you feel about that?"

Again Julia was stunned into silence. Bear ran a finger across her lower lip letting his eyes follow before returning his gaze upon her. "I want you to think about that. Think about how you feel in response to me today. Forget what you think you know and remember what I make you feel."

Julia nodded. "I'll try."

"Trust what your body feels right now. Remember that. Go with that. Okay?" He searched her eyes, waiting for an answer.

"Okay." She agreed, lost in the enormity of what he was asking her to do.

"I'll take that coffee now if you'll come outside with me and enjoy watching the morning sky wake up." He smiled down at her, easing her away from her worries.

"I would like that. Coffee with you and the morning."

Bear pulled her in for a tight hug then and kissed the top of her head. "You'll do fine, Julia." He squeezed her butt in the palm of his hand. "Grannie panties and all."

Julia groaned as she tucked her head into hiding. And then she reached up and pulled his beard.

Bear's laughter echoed, following them all the way down the hall.

TWO CUPS OF coffee into the morning, Bear's phone beeped. Jon asked him to tag along to place a bid on a new job somewhere just on the other side of the Tennessee line. This left Julia to her own plans for the day. Her mission? Lingerie. Something sexy and slinky to go underneath that perfect dress for the Benefit. White and briefs were out of the question. She wanted something that sizzled together with the heels she planned to wear. Bear had instructed her that morning to think about how her body felt when he touched her. Remember the good feelings it told her. Grannie panties did not tell her good things. They reminded her of failure and, if she was honest, made her feel frumpy. So off to Nashville she had gone. And her reward for the trouble? A scrumptious little pink satin thong and matching bra set embellished with the tiniest black bows and even tinier pearls. Her inner woman was proud. Her inner woman was a shock to Julia's system. Her inner woman, it turned out, liked to purr.

By the time Julia made it back to Alabama, the sun was on a race towards evening. She remembered the pair of earrings Angel had suggested to go with the dress, so she headed in the direction of *Angelica's* before going home. Just as she pulled into a parking place, her phone rang.

"Well, my friend, did you find something sinful and delicious to wear under your dress?"

Julia laughed. Her new friendship was a delightful gift in her life. One she was surprised she'd been fortunate enough to receive. "You're almost as bad as Bear is, Christy!"

"Oh? And what are you not telling me? Did I miss something?"

Julia sighed into the phone.

"Uh oh. I *did* miss something! Spill, Jules. Spill!"

Julia laughed at her friend's new name for her. "Jules, is it?"

"Because you're a *jewel,* girlfriend!"

The term made her feel all the more loved. Jules. A friend *and* a nickname, both firsts in her life. Julia shook her head at the wonder of it. "Well, you missed a lot, but I'm not going to give you explicit details."

"What? But . . ." Christy complained.

"I don't work that way, Christy. The details are private. Just between me and Bear." She dropped her shoulders, wincing a little as she did so. "I hope that doesn't offend you. I just can't talk about it with anyone." *Would her new friend understand?*

"It's okay. I completely understand. Really."

Julia relaxed a little, letting her relief wash the concern away. "Let's just say Bear and I are on the same page, shall we?"

Christy's laughter comforted Julia through the phone.

"Well, I can't wait to see the two of you together then."

"Speaking of Bear, have the guys gotten back from their bid yet?" Julia hadn't heard from Bear all day.

"Oh honey, they got back hours ago. Jon's over in Huntsville now on something totally different. Hold on a sec, will you?"

Julia heard Rudi in the background saying something about a puppy.

"Sure honey. Y'all just check in every once in a while, okay sweetheart?"

Peals of laughter and little quipping barks disappeared in the distance over the phone. "Sorry about that. Rudi and Tracie are playing and wanted to go to the park. So anyway, what were we saying?"

"Oh nothing. I was just wondering if Bear and Jon were back is all. I haven't heard from him today."

"Oh. Well, I don't know where he headed when they got back. His truck's still here, but his bike is gone. He'll be back eventually." She laughed.

Julia chewed on her lower lip. "I guess so." She watched as Angel rearranged a display in her front window. Angel waved at Julia when she saw her watching from the car. "If you see him will you ask him to call me, please? I'm hungry. I wanted to see if he wanted to have dinner together."

"Sure. But if you haven't heard from him in an hour or so, drop by. We're firing up the grill out back. There's plenty to share."

Julia laughed at Christy. "You amaze me, my friend. Always ready for a party, aren't you."

"Life's a party, sweetheart! Haven't you figured that out by now?"

They laughed together.

"Okay. I'll be in touch. I've got to run for now, though."

They said their goodbyes then Julia stepped out into the fall air just as Angel was flipping her *Open* sign to *Closed.* Julia took off at a jog to catch her before she left.

Angel saw her coming and opened the door to Julia. She laughed as she folded her arms across her petite body. "You remembered those earrings, didn't you?'

Her smile was infectious. Julia couldn't help but return the warmth. She pushed a piece of hair behind her ear as a blush of pink ran up her neck. "Am I that transparent?"

"Oh, not in the least. I just know those earrings were made for that dress. And your face." She smiled broadly as she escorted Julia into the shop. Scooting around the back of the counter, Angel retrieved the jewelry box she'd set aside for Julia. "I knew you'd be back so I set them behind the counter for you."

Julia laughed. "You're so sure of yourself. How did you ever come by that trait?"

Angel slapped a hand against her chest. "Oh lordy! Please don't ever say that in front of my siblings. They'll never let me hear the end of it!"

"I didn't mean it as a bad thing, really. I meant, how did you ever learn such confidence? You wear it well. Your brother seems to have it, too."

A softness transpired between the two of them as Angel understood what Julia was saying. She slipped back around the counter and close to Julia. "I suppose I've never known anything else but confidence. Confidence and certainty. I had the greatest papa in the world, a mother whom he adored and who loved him back for all to see. I have the best sisters and brother anyone could ever dream of. Mix them all together, throw in the extended family in the mother land and I never had a chance to be anything but confident. They have always been there for me, egging me on and bolstering me up when life tried to pull me down."

"Haven't you ever been down though, beaten or stepped on? Not that it's a good thing. Just that I thought everyone experienced that to some degree. Right?"

"I was, once." Angel let her head fall to her shoulder and sighed. "My big little brother beat the pulp out of the man who broke my heart. Then my sisters packed me up and took me away to Italy for a while to give me time to heal. That's what families do, Julia. They take care of each other. Right?" She reached out and touched Julia's arm, gave her a squeeze. "At least that's what the Grecco family is all about."

Julia nodded. Frowned. "My family wasn't like that."

Angel pulled her into a hug then and pushed her shoulder under Julia's head, patting her back in reassurance. "It's okay, hon. You're with us now."

Noises erupted from the other side of the wall followed by a door slamming.

"What's that all about?"

Angel lifted a shoulder and shrugged. "I guess the moody artist is at work?"

"Ha!" Julia chortled. "They *can* be moody, I'm told."

Minutes later, after Angel wrapped the jewelry and sent Julia on her way, she stepped back out into the evening. Long shadows of the day's end stretched across the pavement of the street. She walked toward her car just as a black curtain slammed across the front of Angel's neighbor's door. *Moody indeed*, she thought before stopping to take a closer look. The display case was empty just as Angel had projected it would be. If appearances were right, the room inside was vacated too, leaving the property abandoned, she assumed. Julia sighed. What a transient life behind those doors. And though it made her sad to think it, she realized she had so much to be thankful for. She was setting down roots with a home and friends, no longer on the run from herself. It was a good feeling. She hugged herself and let the idea wash over her. Yes, just another good feeling Bear gave to her. A feeling of belonging. A feeling of goodness. Before turning to her car, Julia wished the artist a sense of goodness as well. A belonging. A home to light. A place to call his own.

"WELL THAT WAS a close call, little brother." Angel rested a hand over her heart and let her shoulders relax.

"Sorry Angel. I didn't expect to see her drive up while I was emptying the display case."

"You haven't told her who you really are yet, have you?" Concern scattered across her features. "Bear you have to tell her. She can't find out like everyone else."

Nicki, the oldest of the Grecco girls, entered the building through the back door that led from the alleyway. Her hair was dark and long, pulled back into a clip out of her face. She was dressed in jeans and a tee, clearly in work mode and the authority of the bunch. She slapped dust off of her hands. "That's everything going to the show, right? All of these others stay?" She pointed to the stacks still in the room before turning to face Bear and Angel. "And who told who what?" She was the sister heading up the Benefit and not being one to get power minded, she was also part of the labor force, helping Bear transfer his artwork (secretly, of course) to the auction they planned to showcase his work from. Bear was hiding behind anonymity, but Nicki was vested in his secret until the very end and she would not risk compromising the impact of his identity being discovered on *her* project. But even without the event, she would protect her little brother. He was family. Family was bound. "What kind of secrets does Bear have now?" She quirked an eyebrow in his direction.

Bear groaned knowing this would not end well for him. "That stack over by the door goes, too. Everything else stays." Nobody was listening to him. He took his bike and walked it to the door then sat on the piano seat to wait the women out.

"He hasn't told Julia who he really is." Angel turned to Bear. "Hon, she's got to know beforehand. You don't want to scare her away."

"This isn't your mission, Angel." Bear growled.

Nicki pushed up against Bear and put her arm around his shoulder. "Oooh. Do tell, Angel." She grinned at Bear slyly. "Who is this Julia woman?"

My woman bear ground out inside his head. *Mine.* He grunted out loud.

Nicki laughed. "Looks like you got your fur ruffled, buddy."

Angel slapped a hand up on her tiny hip. "He may have his fur ruffled, but if he doesn't come clean with her before the event, she's going to run for a cave and it won't be his." She marked the last few words by poking a finger into Bear's middle. "Be careful with her. She's the keeping kind."

"Whoa. Wait." Nicki stepped away from Bear and faced him directly. "You have a *real* woman, not just some fluff for a night, and I didn't know about it?" She waited for his response impatiently.

Bear grunted again, but before he could say a word Angel piped in. "Not only does he have a woman, and one he's asked to go to the Benefit, but now he's painting that! She pointed at the large canvas leaning against the wall with the woman and child in his landscape. He didn't paint people, women or otherwise. He painted landscapes. Only. People were a first for Bear. "That's her in the painting, Nicki."

Nicki walked back away from the painting to get a good view of the woman. "She's lovely, Bear." She looked at him then, assessing his response to her seeing this woman of his.

"I sold her one of my originals to wear to the event, too." Angel said. "She's very nice, Nicki. You'll like her. She's quiet though. She's soft, not fragile, mind you. She has a delicate heart. Yes, that's it. A delicate heart."

Nicki was all ears then, listening to the details of who Julia was and what she was like. "So how long have you been seeing her, Bear?"

Bear mumbled something and walked to the last stack of canvases by the door, picked them up, shouldered his bike, and moved on toward the truck parked out back.

"What was that? I couldn't understand you?" Nicki's agitation was beginning to show. "Did he say a year?" She looked at Angel for confirmation.

Angel lifted her shoulders. "Don't ask me. He's not talking to me either. Everything I know I found out from Julia and Christy, Jon's wife."

"What the hell? Jon knows and I don't?"

Angel shook her head and threw her hands up in the air. "I don't know how long he's been seeing her. But I know he better tell her who he really is if he wants to keep seeing her."

Nicki took off after Bear as he slipped through the door. "Does Mama know about this? What about the twins? Am I the last one to hear of this?" She was mad and getting madder.

Bear kept a steady pace moving forward, ignoring her.

"Giovanni Columbera Grecco! Stop and talk to me this minute!" The alley door slammed hard behind her leaving Angel out of the mix.

Bear turned and shot a hard look at her.

"I get it." She held up her hands in defense. "None of my business."

"Damn straight." Bear pushed the truck door up and positioned his burden inside.

Nicki marched right up next to him and started fiddling with how he was stacking the works inside, pushing him around and taking charge like she always did. "This *is* my business. This whole event is my business and you better not screw it up. We're in a good place with this big secret of ours. Keep it that way."

Bear pushed her to the side to place his bike inside the interior of the truck so he had a way home after delivering the truck.

"I mean it Bear. Your identity is top secret until I make the introduction from the auction. You got that?"

Bear proceeded to pull the back door down to lock it up, neat and tidy. At that precise moment, the texts started rattling his and Nicki's phones simultaneously. One look told him his secret was out. With the divas, anyway. And oh Lord, Mama Paula was in on it too. They were texting back and forth in a group so fast he just shook his head and turned his phone off. There was only one thing worse than Mama Drama, and that was Diva Drama. He zeroed in on Nicki. "You mind your business. I'll mind mine."

"Bear. . ."

"The truck will be parked at the reception hall, waiting for the morning crew to unload it. You watch your men how they handle my stuff. I won't be there. To protect the secret, of course." He leaned down and kissed her cheek, putting their conversation to a close from his perspective.

Nicki kept talking about women and secrets and . . .

"I'm out." He climbed into the truck, turned the motor over and put it in gear leaving his bossy sister shaking her fist in his dust.

CHAPTER NINE

LITTLE DOGGIE BARKS and laughter
erupted through the air just as Bear pushed through
the back yard gate at Jon and Christy's place.
Rudi's plate crashed to the ground serving up a fine
hot dog for Puff to leap on which elicited more
giggles from Rudi and Tracie.

"What? A party and no one called me?" Bear
threw out into the mix.

"Pshaw! Your truck's here. I figured you'd
show up sooner or later." Jon aimed his bottle at the
cooler by the back porch steps. "Grab yourself a
cold one and I'll throw a dog on the fire for you."

Bear rubbed his stomach and wiped his face off
on his shirt sleeve. "Make it three or five. I'm
hungry."

Julia scooted over on the picnic bench to make
room for him next to her. He swooped in and

planted a sloppy kiss on her right there in front of God and everybody before straddling the bench.

"Ewe gross!" Rudi gave up a gagging imitation. "That's disgusting!" Giggles and more barking followed. "We're going to go play ball with Puff." Off they went away from the adults as far as they could within the fenced yard.

Christy laughed at the girls and walked over to her own man and wrapped her arms around him while he manned the grill.

"So where have you been all day, Princess?" Bear leaned in for another taste of her lips and moaned his delight at the taste of her. Pulling back just enough to speak, "I heard you bought special little things today." A rub of the nose. A last quick nip at the lower lip. "Care to share?"

Julia pushed back at him, surprised and a little bit alarmed. "Who told you that? I haven't seen or told anyone what I did today."

Bear grinned. "Sugar, if there's one thing I know, I know what a woman looks like when she's gone shopping." Bear felt mischievous and didn't mind showing it. "Besides, I have my ways. I know people"

"Uh huh. You know people." She punched him playfully in the arm.

He stretched across her to snag a handful of chips. "I do, it's a fact. I know people all over this town and the town's around here. Right Jon?" They turned to see Jon's response. Clearly the whole situation was lost on him and Christy who were tangled up in their own private sparring of sorts.

Julia laughed out loud.

Bear grinned. "Looks like they followed my lead."

"So, Mr. Smarty Pants. If I've been out shopping all day, what have you been up to?" She smiled into his face.

Bear saw something different in her face tonight. A softness that had been unearthed. And he knew he was responsible for it. He watched her and thought of her pressed against the door early that morning. Lordy, but she tempted him. "Did you do what I asked today?"

Julia lifted a shoulder and shyly responded. "I did."

Her eyes were so telling, he thought. Soft and dewy. Innocent. Enticing.

Julia slipped a hand into his and nestled into his side, hiding her face from his sight. "Tell me, please. What did you do today after working with Jon? Anything special?"

Bear toyed with her fingers and wondered what was going on inside her mind, the specifics. He suspected he knew, but he could wait her out until they were alone. He could respect her need for privacy. "Nothing much. A little of this. A little of that. Checked on Mama Paula. Rode my bike." He leaned back and stretched his arms overhead. "Feeling like the days almost over and I can reward myself with a little something-something."

"Oh yeah? What's that?"

He reached out and slipped his arms underneath her and lifted, cradling her, and pulled her up onto his lap where he could touch her. Having her anchored with one arm, he slipped his other hand over her, resting it on her ribcage to dance little thumb circles along the underside of her breast. "I'm thinking I need to eat and get us out of here fast as lightning." He bent his head and eased his lips around hers.

Julia squirmed a little, warring his public display, but finally gave up, sighed, and let him provoke her. "I think you've got a one track mind."

"Hmm." He squeezed her bottom. "You would be right."

THE EVENING PROVED to be a stellar autumnal event with the moon glowing in the sky and the restless leaves crinkling in the breeze yet refusing to give in to fall. The puppy had worn the girls out which in turn brought the night to a close. Julia found herself being pulled along the way to stretch the night out with one big determined bear with a bicycle thrown over his shoulder. He seemed content to continue on through the night, certain even, that she would accept him.

Julia laughed softly into the night air.

Bear gave her hand a tug and pulled her in close enough to wrap his free arm around her. "What's got you tickled?"

She looked up into his face and smiled. "You." She stopped and reached up to his beard and smoothed her hand over its softness. "You're just so sure of yourself, aren't you?" She winked at him.

Bear reached in and stole a quick kiss then lingered for more.

Julia laughed again before pulling away just far enough to see his face. "See what I mean?"

"What? Can't a guy get a kiss from his girl?" He snuck around her then and began kissing along her neck, tickling her with his beard and eliciting more giggles.

"So I'm *your girl* now, am I?

"Mine." Bear growled playfully before reaching down and pulling her in tight against his hard body.

Julia let him pull her, allowed him to consume her right there in the road to her house for any and all to see. She didn't care anymore. She liked that he wanted her. Reveled in his demand for her. And melted right into his firm body letting him engulf her in passion.

Bear growled again and reluctantly pulled away. "Get us behind closed doors before I do something Dicker is sure to show up for and be witness to."

Julia blinked. His words took a minute to sink in. She touched his face, trying to memorize its shape and form. It was a nice face. Not one she would ever in a million years have thought she would fall for what with the beard and the ponytail adorning it. But she did. She had. She'd fallen hard. Her heart did a little flip upside down and plopped right there in the bottom of her chest. And she knew. She'd fallen for a bear and was completely at his mercy. When realization dawned, she threw her arms out and laughed again. "I give in Mr. Certainty! I'm yours! Take me away."

Bear set his bike to the ground in one muscled movement and mounted it with grace. He aimed his head towards the handlebars and ordered, "Get on."

"What? I can't. . ."

"Just sit on the handles and hold your feet up while I pedal. It'll get us where we want to be, fast." He winked and nodded forward, egging her on.

"Well, alrighty then." She slipped a leg over the front wheel of the bike and sat back carefully on the handlebars. Just as she was situated, Bear took off, gaining speed with her squeals of joy trailing behind them.

As they pulled into the driveway of Julia's house, Bear stopped and she hopped down. She stretched up high to the sky. "That was an unexpected thrill!" She laughed.

Bear wiggled his eyebrows. "If you liked that ride wait until I get you inside, sweetheart."

"Ha! You are incorrigible!" She playfully taunted him as he began hunting her down. "Do you even know how to keep your paws to yourself?"

"Oh I'll get my paws on you, sugar. It's just a matter of a few footsteps now. "

Julia came to a stop as he backed her into the screen door that led inside. She could see playfulness dancing in his eyes as he trapped her. His eyes dipped down and took in her lips. She ran her tongue across them in response, leaving a sheen of silk behind to entice him. Bear made a sound soft and deep in the back of his throat. "You know I want you. I've wanted you since the last second I had you. And I'll keep wanting you even when I'm full. You know that, right?"

Julia nodded. She knew this. Comprehended it the first time she had laid eyes on him last Thanksgiving. But not until this very moment had she even considered allowing herself to want, to desire, to crave with abandon.

"Teach me what you want from me."

Bear didn't move but for the intake of breath.
The air around them gusted and a pile of leaves
thrust into the little portico. Julia kept her eyes on
him, waiting as the moon slipped slowly past.
Sounds of the night came and went, in what seemed
a million years, while Bear seemed to look deep
inside her, pondering, mulling, considering. And
when she thought he'd slip back onto his bike and
ride away into the night, Bear dropped his head and
slipped his mouth to hers, slowly at first then diving
in for what she knew he wanted, needed. Her.

Bear pulled back just far enough for her to hear
him and whispered softly, "This first, but then I
need you more. More of you."

Julia didn't understand what more meant when
you gave all of yourself. But she let it go. And she
let Bear take her where he wanted to go.

SHE DIDN'T KNOW how he did it, but Bear
was intuitive to her home, perfectly comfortable
without any reservation. He came toward her
through the bedroom door carrying a tray, laden
with food and wine and a candle glowing in the
night. The candle only showed her again that the
man was beautiful. Not in the way of models and

movie stars, but in his grace and sinew and power. It was something of how he moved, each movement deliberate and calculated and smooth. And stunning. She realized she was staring and sat up to fluff the pillows around her, making room for him and his feast.

"It's okay to look me over, you know. I do the same to you every chance I get." He slipped in, reached past her to lay the tray in the middle of the bed, and snagged a kiss on his way back. "You're a beautiful woman, Julia." His voice provoked her. He slipped his mouth along her chin and took another kiss from her, letting his wet lips pop as he drew away to rub her nose with his own. "I like beautiful women."

Julia had no idea how to respond. She wasn't beautiful, not in that way. She knew this all too well being as her grandmother had told her often how plain she was.

"Stop thinking of what that old biddy filled your head with."

"What? Who . . .?"

Bear moved to sit on the edge of the bed and reached across her body to anchor himself. "I know your grandmother filled you with her twisted perspective on life, Julia. Surely someone has told you how beautiful you are before now?" He frowned.

Julia fumbled with the hem of the sheet. "Bear, you don't have to say these things to entice me. You've already had me." She shook her head shyly to the side without looking up. "I know I'm no supermodel, so please don't say those things to me."

Bear reached a hand under her chin and lifted. She couldn't hide her eyes from him or the threat of tears his words incited. Compassion poured out from him. "Julia, I don't say things I don't mean. *You* are the most beautiful woman I have ever known." He sighed. "Just look at how I've trailed after you like a sick puppy all this time. I don't trail after anyone. Women throw themselves at me all the damn time."

Julia tried to look away, embarrassed at being the topic of their discussion but Bear pulled her back in with his hand and held her in his sight. His skin was warm and he soothed her cheek with his caress. "I can't imagine why you've followed me like you have." She laughed without humor. "I'm nobody, Bear. I'm not pretty. I don't have money," she lifted a shoulder in defeat, "anymore anyway. I'm not smart or particularly stylish." The tears started a slow trail down her cheek and she laughed out loud. "And I can't seem to hold the tears back either. Geesh!" She rolled her eyes at herself and groaned. "God I thought I was past this."

Bear pulled her forward then with both hands behind her head and kissed her softly letting his thumbs brush against her face with care and tenderness. Before he pulled back he nuzzled her face with his own, leaving a trail of tender kisses along the way.

"You're beautiful to me." Bear nodded slowly, and paused before forging ahead. "When I look at you I see a woman of so many different wonderful parts. Sure, maybe each part on its own isn't the most beautiful in the world. I mean you have a nice enough shoulder," he kissed it and smiled tenderly. "But I'm sure there's a shoulder out there that's insured by Lloyds of London for its incredible beauty and perfection." He moved his hand from her shoulder to her hand. "Same with your fingernails or your kneecaps." Each place he mentioned, he followed with a kiss. "And your mind, well, you're smart in all the important ways. Smart enough to teach the kids. That's a good thing, Julia. Not everyone is cut out for teaching. It's an important thing you do with the children in our community." He nodded, letting her see his words were genuine. "But then there's that crazy Einstein guy who's so smart he makes us all look a fool." He chuckled. "So you're right. You probably don't have any life-changing formulas to shake the world up with for the next few centuries." A deep concentration appeared on his forehead. Quiet engulfed them. Time passed as he gathered his thoughts. He looked at her again and let his intensity fade a little. He sat up straighter and continued. "But here's the thing, Julia. You take all of those ordinary parts you have that are nice enough but not perfect, mix them all together in your own unique and lovely way, and what have you got?" Again he reached a hand to her face, moving it around to showcase her features. "You are a masterpiece, Princess. You are lovely and beautiful in your own wonderful way." He closed the distance between them and set his lips to hers in the gentlest way, sighing into her lips, and sealing his words to her heart. Julia let him wash over her. She had craved just this her whole life. Every inhibition had been fueled by the lack of this communion with another. She basked in the healing he offered. His words, if true, were like the finest stitches of a great surgeon, artistry performed on the canvas of her heart.

Bear pulled away from her and feasted his eyes on her again. "That's the beauty I see." He ran a hand down her arm, leaving goose bumps in its wake. "The whole is greater than the sum of its parts. Isn't that what some famous philosopher said?"

Julia enveloped herself in his tenderness. "I don't know. I guess so. Maybe Aristotle?"

"That's you. That's precisely your beauty. And you've got heart. That's what makes you shine. Not everybody has that, you know." He nodded his head, thinking and confirming his own words to himself. "Yup. The entirety of you is greater than all of your individual parts, sugar." He took her hand and lifted it to his lips. "And I can't seem to get enough of your beauty."

Julia heard him, his words. Emotions threatened to push them away, but she tapped them down and held his thoughts tight, wanting to comprehend, craving to believe him. When she could find words of her own, she spoke, trying to lighten the mood. "Well, if it's all about my kneecaps, well then, there is that."

Bear didn't blink. "Don't discount my words, Julia."

Julia dropped her chin. "I'm sorry, Bear." She twisted her fingers around the sheet. "I didn't mean . . ." She breathed in deeply and gathered her courage to look up and into his eyes. "No one has ever told me that I am beautiful. Not once that I can ever remember." Her voice was quiet, soft. "It makes me uncomfortable to hear this." Suddenly she sat straighter. "Don't get me wrong. I want to hear it. Hearing it from you makes it even better." She watched his expression and when she was sure he understood, she leaned back into the pillows for support. "It's just that it's not an easy thing for me to believe." Her eyes begged him to understand. "All I can remember ever being told were my failures, my missteps, and my inability to measure up. Grandmother's standards are a bit unattainable, if you know what I mean."

Bear reached in and once again kissed her tenderly. "Why don't you tell me more about your world and let me decide?"

"My world is boring, fraught with endless charades of foolishness."

"That sounds more like your grandmother's words and I don't want to hear that."

"What do you want to hear?"

Bear stood and walked around the bed and sat back down on the other side, lifting a glass to her as he took one for himself. "I want to hear the sounds of you eating so you have energy for activities I have planned for later." He grinned wide and wiggled his eyebrows causing Julia to laugh again. "While you're eating, I want to hear more about you. Like I said earlier, I need to know more about my woman."

"Such as?"

"For starters, what did you mean when you said you're not rich anymore?" He slipped a grape into his mouth and waited.

"Oh. You caught that, did you?" Again, Julia slumped and fiddled. She drew in a deep breath and decided now and Bear were as good a time and person to share her life with. At least he was asking. "Are you sure you want to know?"

Bear handed her a piece of cheese. "I want you to let me inside your life. I want you to open up and be with me."

"Most people don't want to know, they just want what's in it for them. At least that's what I've experienced." She took a bite and waited for him to change his mind.

"I won't push you to divulge anything you're not willing to. Like I said before, I won't take anything you aren't willing to give. That goes across all categories, sugar. But I would like for you to give and share and lean on me. Let me see the tarnished parts that make the beautiful parts shine so brightly, will you?" He smiled at her reassuringly. "Besides. I'm big. I can take you leaning on me."

Julia wasn't certain, but she felt pressure slip off her shoulders at his asking her to open up to him. She felt a wave of relief, even. Finally someone saw her and understood her even though she hadn't shared a thing. "Okay, if you're sure." She eyed him, still giving him time to back out. But Bear burrowed deep into pillows and pulled the tray close from which to feed her. He lifted his glass, tipped it in her honor, and offered encouragement to carry on.

"Okay then, I'm just going to give you the high points and if you have questions you can ask. Good enough?"

"Sounds good to me. But eat this first." He slipped a grape between her lips.

And so she filled him in on her parents' untimely death when she was in her senior year in high school and how that prompted her to move in with a friend to finish out the year with her peers in Nashville. How Nashville was close enough for her grandmother's heavy influence, which was how she came to be controlled by Mrs. Thurston throughout her college years. And the inheritance that her parents had the foresight to provide had been left for Mrs. Thurston to oversee until Julia turned twenty five. Of course, Mrs. Thurston being, well, Mrs. Thurston, was as tyrannical in the affairs of money as she was in everything else in life. Mrs. Thurston's one soft spot was Julia's brother, Lance. Because, as Julia was reminded more times than she could count, he was just like Julia's father, excellent in every area of life. He was perfect. Unlike Julia. Of course, Julia didn't have thieving down to perfection like he did. A good thing, that. But Lance was his father's namesake, Lance Maurice Thurston, III. Their father was of course the perfect replica of the original Lance Maurice Thurston, Mrs. Thurston's husband whom she adored. But sadly, the senior Thurston never made it to the age of thirty, leaving Mrs. Thurston to raise their son on her own. Julia was berated time after time that she took after *that woman's* side of the family. *That woman* being Julia's mother, the one from somewhere up north who *had no polish about herself at all,* and was solely responsible for taking Julia's father away from his mother. But to Mrs. Thurston's thinking, the Lord had seen fit to give her the gift of Lance III to finish raising. Because being four years Julia's junior, and Mrs. Thurston their guardian, Lance III had been forced to move to Riverland, Alabama, with his grandmother.

So everything that had happened to Julia since her parents' death had been in some way influenced by her grandmother's hold on her life via her inheritance, her brother, and a reflection of Mrs. Thurston's contempt for Julia's mother. Even Julia's college education had been decided upon by Mrs. Thurston, else she would've gotten her degree in something entirely different. Textile arts would have been Julia's preference. But according to Mrs. Thurston, textile arts *did not provide one with a sensible job.*

There was never any question asked of Lance's sensible career. He didn't have one. He had his money, her money, and he had run off to someplace far, far away. And wouldn't it just be fitting if he was somewhere up north. Not that her mother's side of the family deserved him. But they would protect him, for his mother's sake. Because everyone except Mrs. Thurston had loved Julia's mother.

CHAPTER TEN

BEAR SLIPPED A key into the old door of the market and eased in through the back alleyway, sure no one would see him at this late hour. Or was two in the morning an early hour? Whatever. He closed the door behind him and flipped the light switch on. The smell of paint and linseed oil filled his nostrils like it had every other time since he'd discovered it in his youth. He took a minute and drank it into his lungs, like every other time he'd come through that door in past years. It was his place, his retreat, his cave.

He stepped over and placed his bike against the wall, before moving to the far side of the room where his work in progress leaned against the wall. Slipping his hand through his hair and rearranging his ponytail, Bear took in the colors of his work. Nicki was right. Julia was lovely. It was turning into his favorite work of all. But then, so was Julia. His favorite woman of all.

This painting was similar to several he'd already sold, but for the first time in his career, he'd painted a family into the landscape. His family. The one he would have with Julia. It was a nice addition to his portfolio. A good addition. Like he'd been waiting for just the right time to embrace the topic into his work.

A young child pumped her feet up into the air trying to take flight in her rope swing as her father looked on smiling, maybe even laughing. A woman stood a bit further in the distance, leaned over and picked flowers from a garden near a house. The Italian inspired countryside surrounded them and seemed to encourage them to embrace life, giving up its fruit and vegetation as reward. The whole work had a good feeling to it. He liked it. And he knew it would never be for sale. It was his gift for Julia. It was for their home, their manifesto.

Bear judged the size of the canvas and considered what to add. The painting was too big for any easel, like most of his works these days, so he simply picked up his supplies and began painting the oversized piece against the wall. As he painted and added a wisp of wind through the outlying trees in view, Bear thought on Julia and what she'd confided in him earlier. He knew she was a private person and giving up such details exemplified a trust he'd earned with her. Never in his wildest dreams had he thought such details would make him so angry. Which was why he was here painting in this moment. How on earth could a man, any man, family or not, think it right to slip into a person's private papers and accounts and take what didn't belong to them. Bad enough if he'd taken just one thing that didn't belong to him, but this. Taking a password to a banking account had pre-meditation written all over it. Her brother *meant* to take her property and steal her blind. That was unacceptable. But even worse, that old grouch Mrs. Thurston thought it was all right for him to take it, that he deserved it more than Julia simply because he had the smarts *to* take it. Well, that was not going unaddressed if he ever had an open door to speak his mind. The old bat. What would she do if someone came in and stole her privacy? Her passwords? Her belongings?

Bear shut the anger down so as not to let it corrupt the painting in front of him and reflected on tucking his woman in for the night. He'd worn her out, emotionally and physically. But he knew she needed both so she could get over her past and on with her life. The look of sleep drifting over her was almost enough to make him crawl back into her bed and wrap up with her for the night. But he needed space to think and work out his anger. Plus, he wanted to finish this painting so it was ready for his big plan. So he'd tucked her in, left her a note by the coffeepot that simply read…

Couldn't sleep. Out for a ride.

He continued to paint and let his mind work through how he could help Julia without overstepping his welcome. He wanted to see her succeed. He did not want to cause her to digress into self-loathing because he had taken care of her business, as if she couldn't do it herself. He was certain she could handle anything that came her way. He just wanted to assist in some way. He remembered Mama Paula talking nonsense about him hiring a private detective and that gave him an idea. Maybe he should hire a private detective to find her brother or her money? Huh. Something to consider. Certainly, better thinking about that than having Julia followed around by a PI to learn about her. He was doing just fine learning everything he could about her on his own!

Bear continued working through the night. After cleaning his tools, he slipped under a blanket in the storeroom upstairs and dreamed of Julia with a little girl following her around a flower garden with laughter shadowing their every move. Damned if he didn't wake up reaching out, hoping to find her next to him in bed.

THE REST OF Fall Break sped by, filled with every bit of harvest time fun imaginable. Bear and Julia teamed up with Christy and Jon on an excursion to the local pumpkin patch where Rudi and Tracie entertained them with their antics. Even Tracie's mom Donna joined in the fun, taking pictures to record the festivities for her husband Mark to enjoy. After a hay ride through the fields of pumpkins, they had all picked out pumpkins to take home for carving. Of course, that prompted Christy to plan another get together for pumpkin pie. She was all about inviting them back for another day to share the yum. There had been talk of Halloween costumes and shopping followed shortly after. So by the time Sunday rolled around, Julia was rejuvenated by her short vacation and ready to get back to work. Christmas was just around the corner, after all. And she had lots to do with her students to make learning fun for them.

As Julia prepared for her week ahead, Bear left her to her projects and headed out on a ride through the evening air. In the time since Julia opened up to him he'd done a little investigative work trying to find out what had become of her brother, his whereabouts and his state of life. He wanted his woman safe, is all. He had no intent of messing with the man. It wasn't his place. But she was his and he would watch out for her.

JULIA AWOKE TO find herself alone early Monday morning, save for the note left on Bear's pillow.

Good morning, Princess. I couldn't sleep again, so I'm off for a long morning ride. Enjoy your first day back on the job. Love those kids up like I know you do. I'll check on you later.

He signed the note with the drawing of a crown like the one on his wrist.

What a fascinating man. A man that she loved with all of her heart. She sent out a request to the heavens, asking that she get to keep her bear as she traced the crown signature with her fingertip. *Why did he get a tattoo when he insists on covering it up with a watch all the time?* She would try to encourage him to wear it proudly, uncovered.

When Julia sent the kids off to computer lab mid-morning with another teacher, she had a block of time to work and prepare for upcoming lessons. Of course, being the over achiever she was, her lessons were already in order through Christmas and beyond. So what she ended up with was too much time to second guess herself and think.

She wasn't so sure she should've unlocked all the information about her brother to Bear the week before. She'd never told anyone other than her therapist. Of course, her therapist had told her she should tell someone she trusted other than her grandmother about the situation. She'd thought about telling Christy, but Christy never seemed to need to know the personal details of Julia's life, the whys and wherefores. She was just Christy. A good friend. A great friend even, because she accepted Julia on face value with no strings or judgments or expectations beyond friendship.

Now that Bear knew, would his behavior change toward her? Would he try to jump in and treat her like she wasn't able to handle her own life like her family so often did? It was kind of late to worry about that, now. His actions would tell. So far, he hadn't said anything else about it. But then, they had been so busy since she'd told him everything about her past. If his word was true, he'd prove himself by the time the leaves were off the trees for winter. At least that's what he'd said in the beginning. Christy had teased her and told her it wouldn't take him that long. She said bears were incredibly quick at getting what they wanted.

Julia's phoned buzzed.

Thanks for all the Fall Break fun and helping me get to know Donna better. Great things are happening with the girls. Besties are in the make! :D

Julia smiled at her friend's text before responding.

You seem to be in the business of besties! Making one out of me, you are! :D

Julia hit "send" and walked around her classroom placing papers on the desks so the kids could get started on their math worksheets as soon as they returned. She filed the leftovers in her desk drawer just as her phone beeped again.

You're a great bestie! Have an awesome first day back. I'll bet a bear will be waiting at your door after the day is done. <3

Julia couldn't help but laugh at her friend's poking at her.

*You don't fool me anymore, Bestie! I know
you're in cahoots with him! :D*

Before hitting send, she glanced out the school
window, mesmerized into a daydream by the beauty
of the softly falling leaves. She remembered how
Jon oftentimes worked from home and imagined
him standing at the door of his truck looking toward
his house, as if he was waiting for something.

*Go kiss your man...I'll bet he's looking for a
mid-morning piece of you. <3*

Send.

There. Two could play funzies. That's what
friends were for, right? As if to confirm her
thoughts, a big fat *thumbs up* dinged on her phone.
Nothing else, just the thumbs up from her brand
new bestie. And Julia went back into her day feeling
happy, maybe for the first time in her adult life. She
had a bestie. And a big bear-man, too!

CHAPTER ELEVEN

BEAR CAREFULLY CLOSED the door behind him as he entered the old church building on Wednesday night. Singing died down and someone began to pray to close out the evening ceremonies. He spotted Mr. Joe sitting near the back where Mrs. Thurston was in clear view, of course. He was always watching over her.

Bear slipped into the pew next to him and nodded a salutation to Mr. Joe when the man looked up. Bear settled himself and scanned the room to get his bearings of who was in attendance. He recognized a boy sitting just ahead of him on the left side of the aisle, wiggling. The boy fit the description Rudi gave of her classmate. Booger seemed a fitting name, Mischief a suited middle name. He looked like he was up to no good, eyes darting around, watching for the right time and opportunity for trouble.

It hadn't taken much effort to find out which church Mrs. Thurston attended. For all her bossy ways, everyone in the county seemed to know all about her in return. She sat up ahead of him, tall in her seat as the self-appointed matriarch of Riverland, Alabama. She had to. Everyone else knew Lurain Rivers was the true royalty in town, in heart and otherwise. But people were people and Mrs. Thurston was taking what she claimed belonged to her, if for no success but in her own mind.

When the last amen was spoken, Mr. Joe turned to Bear and shook his hand. "You just keep popping up in the least expected places these days, son."

Bear smiled and nodded. "I see you're manning your post." He aimed his head in the direction of Mrs. Thurston.

Mr. Joe acknowledged him by kicking his chin in the same direction. "The woman's a hazard to her own self. Somebody has to watch out for her." He smiled, but a certain sadness laced his face.

"Mr. Joe," Bear spoke quietly so no one around would hear him, "when are you going to step up and take what you want?"

Mr. Joe looked at him, stunned. He sputtered, trying to respond.

"You don't fool me. Maybe you've fooled most everyone else around here, but not me." Bear looked his elder in the eye. "What is it that keeps you always the man next door?"

Mr. Joe sighed heavily and wiped the back of his hand across his face. Clearly this was not something he was comfortable talking about. He scrubbed his thighs with his hands, still trying to find his words.

Bear leaned back in his seat, stretched his legs out as far as he could with the pew in front of him. He wanted Mr. Joe to know he could wait all night long for an answer. He didn't say anything. He just sat there, waiting.

Booger took off running towards the front of the sanctuary, bumping into Mrs. Thurston hard enough to get her attention. She started reprimanding him, but he got away. So she turned and found his father and gave him the business instead, going on and on about some such thing as manners and rules, of course.

"Look at her. She's always got to be the one in charge, that one." Mr. Joe sagged a little.

Bear grunted.

"She's all about telling me no. No I can't mow her yard. No I can't bring her the morning newspaper. No she won't have dinner with me."

"Is *that* why she was always standing at the curb waiting on me to deliver her paper all those years?"

Mr. Joe turned and nodded. "She's afraid of what people will think."

Bear acknowledged him. Nodded. Thought. Bear, still speaking softly, added a measure of kindness to his voice. "How long have you known her?"

Mr. Joe shook his head. "Aw son. The question is, how long *haven't* I known her. I can't even remember the first time we laid eyes on each other, she and I." He leaned up and placed his hands over the pew in front of him and turned his head so Bear could hear his story. "See, her parents were friends with my folks. We go back all the way to birth, I suppose." He tapped the seat ahead of him gently. "She's always been a bit persnickety, even throughout our schooldays. But when her husband died. . ." He trailed off in thought.

"So you knew her husband, then?"

Mr. Joe nodded. "Briefly. I went away for a while and when I came home he was gone. Took a risk and crossed a railroad track late one night in his car, trying to outrun the train to get home, I think it was said."

Bear audibly breathed in, said something under his breath that told of his shock, and crossed his arms over his broad chest to hear the rest.

"She's been like this ever since." They both looked on as the woman gave Booger's father an earful. Mrs. Thurston had her finger pointing in the father's face, pressuring him to take charge of his son's "rearing."

"Losing someone you love can twist a person up inside. It certainly makes you realize how short life is." He turned back to Mr. Joe and spoke. "I know I felt some of that when my Papa died."

Mr. Joe agreed. "Your Papa was good man, son."

"I know that. But I also had my whole life with him, all of it full of happiness, too. Mrs. Thurston didn't get that, not with her husband, anyway. I can't speak for her son."

Mr. Joe shook his head side to side. "Her boy didn't get it either. He got *that* kind of behavior. Right there." Mr. Joe aimed his nose at Mrs. Thurston's tirade.

"So she was alone. Her and her son, fending for themselves. I think she must have been afraid." Mr. Joe didn't respond, he just listened, intrigued by Bear's words.

Bear smoothed the hair around his mouth, away from his lips. "Fear's an ugly beast, Mr. Joe. It'll make people do things, crazy things, things they never planned on being a part of." He made eye contact with Mr. Joe. They nodded their agreement to one another. Bear unfolded himself and leaned over, resting his arms on his legs, letting his hands dangle between his knees. He took in more air than necessary, for strength to forge ahead. "It seems to me her fears are what's telling you no." He looked at Mr. Joe then and felt for the man. "Julia did the same thing to me for a year." Bear waited, but the man remained quiet. "I got fed up with that business."

Mr. Joe continued to listen, but he looked more puzzled with each word Bear spoke.

Bear carried on, "She's mine now, you know. I'm keeping her for good if she'll have me."

Mr. Joe smiled wide and chuckled. "That's the best news I've had in a long time. I'm glad for you son. Really, glad." He slapped Bear on the shoulder congratulating him.

Bear relished the man's sentiment before leaning back where Mr. Joe could see him again. "But Mr. Joe, here's the thing. The way I see it? Julia *couldn't* say yes to me. It wasn't even possible before now because she didn't know how."

Mr. Joe's eyes were focused solely on Bear now, waiting.

Bear shook his head. "Don't you see? Mrs. Thurston doesn't know how to say yes, either."

Mr. Joe's eyes grew big and round. He turned and looked in her direction, pondering the words Bear spoke.

"Go get your woman, Mr. Joe. She's waited long enough."

Mr. Joe turned back to him, astonished. "I never thought about it that way before."

"You just go and do whatever it takes to get her to say yes." Bear winked at him then. "I have every confidence you know just the right thing to do to get her attention." Bear looked for Mrs. Thurston then, assessing the progress of saying her goodbyes for the night. "You think about that and make it happen, okay Mr. Joe? Life's too short to be a spectator."

Mr. Joe nodded, letting the shock of Bear's profound understanding wash over him.

"I've got some business with her now. Sit tight. I won't be long." Bear stood to move away, but turned back at the last minute, worry crossing his face. "Be ready to catch her Mr. Joe. I'm about to give her some hard news. News she's going to need a friend to help her work through."

Bear left Mr. Joe, who now sat on point watching and waiting, and ambled up to Mrs. Thurston. He meant to do a little housecleaning and some mending of the past so the future could take root and grow into something better than before.

MRS. THURSTON HAD no trouble telling him she was surprised to see him in the Lord's house. Bear just let the old war between Protestant and Catholic go, knowing it was a tactic she used to back him away.

"Mrs. Thurston, I want you to know I've been seeing your granddaughter."

She huffed. "Good luck with that one," she sneered, her disappointment in Julia visible.

"I thought you should know that I'm serious about her."

Mrs. Thurston waved him off like she couldn't be bothered and tried moving past him. Bear knew how to use his body strength as good as she did her weakness of character and refused to let her pass. Defiance fueled her and she aimed it up at him directly, staring him down.

"I'm so serious about her that I've done a bit of a background check."

A rod shot up her back then, making her stand at full attention. "Oh?"

Bear placed his nose between his thumb and forefinger, squeezed and hoped for this to go well. He resigned himself, stood as tall as she insisted from herself and began a trek into the land of discomfort.

"Mrs. Thurston, come with me." They walked stiffly away from the few remaining folks talking and laughing with one another. After putting a fair amount of distance between them, Bear looked for Mr. Joe and nodded, encouraged by his watchful eye. "Mrs. Thurston, I know about the unfortunate events of Julia's inheritance." She seemed unruffled by this announcement. "I also know where your grandson is, now. Today."

Everything but Bear faded to the background in that moment for Mrs. Thurston. She was clearly all ears, hanging on his next words.

The information Bear was about to expose to her, no one was ever prepared to hear about their loved ones. "I know he went to Mexico when he left here, but he also returned shortly thereafter. See. . ." he looked at the old stained glass windows that showed a dove in flight. He had to change direction and help her understand what he was about to reveal to her. "He didn't have much respect for life after his parents died, did he?"

Mrs. Thurston deflated a bit. She nodded. "No. I don't suppose he did. Losing his father broke him."

"Ruined him, you mean."

Mrs. Thurston gasped in horror. Bear held his ground. Her stature stooped a little more under the weight of her sadness. Loss was a heavy mantle to carry. And for the first time he saw how fragile she really was. The world had weighed on her for so very long. He understood her pain. It had taken a harsh toll on her, beating at her year after year. Mr. Joe's revelation of her husband made it all clear in his mind. And Bear's heart hurt for her. He reached out and took her hands into his own feeling he had to soften this for her so she could withstand yet another blow of hurt. "Mrs. Thurston, I'm very sorry to tell you, but Lance was found a while back."

She slanted her head, frowned. "Found? What do you mean, found?"

Bear squeezed her hands. "Here. Let's sit down for a minute so I can explain." Bear extended his hand to assist her as she lowered herself to the nearest pew. Mr. Joe stood in the distance, ready to step in and save her. Bear gave him a look of approval and turned back to carefully lay out the details for Mrs. Thurston.

"I hired an investigator to find Lance. He gave me his report just this afternoon. I felt you needed to know right away. And before you start denying what I'm about to tell you, I checked it out with the local authorities before believing it myself."

Mrs. Thurston nodded, though still a bit reluctant.

"They verified everything the investigator reported to me."

Satisfied so far, she pursed her lips, braced to take what he had to say. "Go on."

"The information I was given by the investigator. . ." Bear stopped then, needing to explain his position. "Please understand, I only meant to find Lance so I could protect Julia, help her put this behind her. It's not like I set out to discover this, Mrs. Thurston. I never wanted to find this, you understand." Mrs. Thurston nodded. "Lance was found in his apartment in Cleveland by his landlord. He hadn't paid the rent on time and she went looking for him. When he didn't answer the door, after a week went by, she used her keys to go in and that's when she found him. No one stepped up to claim him as family. He left no contact information for next of kin when he rented the apartment."

Mrs. Thurston was stunned, but quiet. Unresponsive as yet.

"The authorities tried to locate his family for months before the decision was made to bury him." Bear stopped talking. He gave her time to think before giving her the rest of what he knew.

Mrs. Thurston bowed her head. She clasped her hands together and sagged as the news settled in. She sniffed, giving evidence of her grief.

Mr. Joe arrived, kindly offering her a handkerchief.

Mrs. Thurston looked at Mr. Joe and accepted his generosity, thanked him, even. "Is that all, Bear?

Is that everything you found out?" She blotted her nose with the cloth, waiting for his response.

Bear shook his head. "No. Not quite all of it. His landlord did away with all of his belongings except for his wallet. All that was in it was his first and last name and a key. There wasn't even a driver's license. No money. Just the key. And his name. The PI found that it belonged to a safe deposit box at a bank near his house. I thought maybe he put Julia's money there." Again he shook his head. Mrs. Thurston watched for news of something good. Something hopeful. "The only thing inside the box was a stack of papers, things he'd written. Letters to you, to Julia. Memories of his parents and life from his childhood. Happy times. Some poetry. And a photo of himself and Julia when they were in their teens, laughing together."

"Before the accident."

Bear watched, waiting for her to give him hell or instructions of what to do next. She did neither. Tears just ran down her face. When her shoulders began to shake Mr. Joe stepped around the pew and sat with her, wrapping his arms around her and letting her lean on someone other than herself. Bear thought how unfortunate, to have lived and lost most everyone you had loved throughout your lifetime and still have to breathe day in and day out without them. How horrible that particular hell must be.

"Mrs. Thurston." Bear took her hand into his and willed her some strength. "I cannot begin to understand your pain and loss. I won't even pretend I do."

She sniffled, unladylike but uncaring of her surroundings.

"But Mrs. Thurston." He waited for her to look him in the eye. He needed to know she was with him when he said the next thing he had to say.

"Yes. Go on." She sat up the tiniest bit, giving her all to pay him what was left of her mind.

"You still have two people alive and deserving of your love." He looked at Mr. Joe then and let her follow his sight.

Mr. Joe gave her shoulders a squeeze. "I'm here Ivy. I'll always be here."

She sobbed out a cry then, recognizing him maybe for the first time. He pulled her in closer and let her cry.

Bear didn't want to interrupt their moment, but he had one more detail to handle and he wasn't leaving until it was done. So he sat and waited. The pastor got his attention and, showing his concern, offered his assistance. Bear indicated with his expression that he and Mr. Joe had it under control. So the pastor gave them their privacy and left them in the sanctuary alone.

After a few minutes of crying, Mrs. Thurston pulled away from Mr. Joe and attempted to clear throat. Her voice was shaky and small when she finally spoke. "I assume, since you're still here that is, that there's more to tell me."

Mr. Joe was a wall of strength in full protective mode. He gave Bear the look of don't-you-mess-with-my-woman. Surely he knew exactly what Bear meant to do.

Bear acknowledged his authority and carried on. "With all due respect, ma'am. You still have one grandchild that very much needs your appreciation and love. She is broken hearted, too." Bear held Mrs. Thurston's eyes to his own. "She needs your love and approval. She always has."

She wiped at her face with her hands, the handkerchief of no use anymore, and sighed, leaning her back into Mr. Joe's arms. "You're right, Bear. I've not handled my granddaughter well. I've been abominable to her always siding with the child I thought needed me more." She dropped her head in despair and twisted her hands. "I don't know. Does she know all of this yet? Did you tell her already?"

Bear frowned. "No. For some reason I can't wrap my head around, I thought it was important to tell you first."

"Well then, let me tell her, will you? Will you give me that, please?" She looked away towards the altar, ashamed. "Though, after all this time, I can't imagine why she would forgive me. Or that she even could."

Bear patted her hand, regaining her attention. "Give it a try, will you?" He looked behind her for assistance. "You'll help her out, right, Mr. Joe?"

Mr. Joe's face spread as wide as it would go. "It would be my honor to assist Ivy."

Bear grinned back at the pair. "I think you underestimate just how big people can love, Mrs. Thurston. I think you'll be pleasantly surprised." He winked at her and turned to Mr. Joe. "You make sure she gets home safe and sound, all right?"

"Go on, Bear. I've got this one under control." Mr. Joe winked back at him, and without letting Ivy Thurston in on their secret, gave Bear a big thumbs up behind her back.

CHAPTER TWELVE

THURSDAY AFTERNOON, JULIA started
her car and put it into gear. She'd spent the last half
hour letting Angel make sure the alterations of her
dress were perfect what with the benefit only a few
days away now. Just as she pulled away from the
curb a flash of bike whizzed around the corner of
the building and caught her attention. Was that
Bear? She made a quick U-turn and pulled into the
alley next to the old market building. The back door
was open to the old market, so she parked under a
tree that looked to have been planted to mark a spot
for someone years ago, and jumped out of her car to
catch up with him. She knocked and called out to
Bear at the open door, but there was no response.
Looking through the doorway, she could see his
bike leaning against the wall, so she cautiously let
herself in. The smells of paint and linseed invaded

her senses, but the vision behind the door caught her breath such that she backed away from it and slid down the wall to sit next to the bike. What lay in front of her was unbelievable. She let her eyes take in its beauty. The scenery. The people. The skill it had been produced with was unimaginable. Finally she let her eyes wander around the room. Canvas after canvas were stacked neatly around the perimeter of the space. The only furniture pieces were a stool and easels of various sizes. No drop cloths or extra accessories. Just paints and brushes, easels and canvases. And the one huge painting leaning against the opposite wall, a masterfully executed scene of Skyline Mountain with a view of her own house perched above the trailhead. A family mingled among blossoming trees in its landscape; man watching a young girl laughing from a tree swing, a woman picking flowers, a Moses Basket carrying a resting baby nearby. The woman's attentive smile was aimed at the basket. Julia could hear inside her head the sounds of baby cooing its special sounds to his mother. *Giocco* scrolled across the bottom right-hand corner with the stamp of a familiar crown. The tattoo. Bear's tattoo. And for all the magnificent beauty and love portrayed before her, the only thing she felt was the blow to her heart. He'd betrayed her. Never once had he told her that he was *Giocco*. *The Giocco*. The one and only world-renowned *artiste*. She'd finally thought she could trust someone with her heart again and that one person she'd dared to trust betrayed her. Her eyes filled with tears as the grip of hurt squeezed her heart. What a fool she'd been. An utter fool! Again! She sucked in a breath and stood. And then it hit her. She'd thought less of him like everyone had thought of her. She'd given out exactly what she had been given, precisely what she'd vowed never to do to another human being for as long as she lived. How many times had she complained of his apparent laziness and commented on his lack of initiative yet he had never once behaved that way with her. She remembered how he'd coached her one morning after their first night, encouraged her and pulled her to believe what she knew to be true and what she herself had experienced with him rather than what she assumed of him, mainly due to his appearance. She'd poured it on deep to the one least deserving of her harsh judgment. She had to get out of there before he found her. She had to go. Run. Somewhere. Panic overtook her and she scrambled out the door only to run head on into the wall of a man. Bear grabbed her by the shoulders to steady her. She wouldn't let him see her break down like this. She just couldn't. So she wrangled out of his hands and took off running as hard and fast as she could toward her car. Bear ran after her, calling for her to stop. But she leapt into her car, hit the locks and drove away leaving him in her dust.

Just then Angel stepped out of the back of her store, curious. "Bear? Is everything okay?"

Bear threw his hands on top of his head in distress and kicked at the gravel. All he had was his bike. He couldn't even chase Julia down. He didn't have a clue where she'd go. Who would she turn to? And he hadn't told her about her brother, either. *Idiot!* He roared inside. Then he shot towards Angel. "Keys! Now!"

Angel shook her head. "Oh Bear! You never told her, did you?"

"Just give me the damn keys to your car, Angel. I have to go," he bellowed. "*Now!*"

"Go! They're in the ignition!"

Bear landed in the driver's seat and spun out in the direction of the mountain before his door even closed.

"Find her, Bear!" Angel mouthed in his wake. And she looked to heaven and said a prayer for her baby brother.

JULIA DROVE LIKE a crazy woman desperate to think of someplace to go where no one would find her. She finally remembered and headed to just the right place. No one would ever think of her grandmother's house on Elm Street. She'd park behind the house so no one could see her car. Maybe her grandmother could behave like family for once in her life. Or not. She didn't deserve anything better than a beating right now and she'd take the hidey hole for what it was, the place she was most *unlikely* to be found. It would at least give her time to sort it out and make a plan.

When she flew into the kitchen by way of the back door, her grandmother visibly gasped and just about lost her teacup in surprise. "Lordy, child! What has gotten into you?"

Julia's eyes darted here and there, tear stains running down her face.

"Julia!" Her grandmother began showing concern. "Honey what's the matter? You look. . ."

"Grandmother, I need time."

"Time? Time for what?" Her face scrunched up in question. "Julia you're hysterical. Calm down and make sense, child!"

"It's Bear. He lied." Julia ran to the living room and peeked out through the draperies toward the street.

"Lied? Whatever did he lie to you about?"

Julia looked at her grandmother. *Oh God, please have mercy on me. Let her keep her horrible judgments to herself today. Please, God. Please?*

151

"Well, not lied, really, just withheld, I guess." She headed down the hallway and checked the windows in the bedroom toward Mr. Joe's house.

Mrs. Thurston was right behind her, breathing down her neck. "What? He promised me he wouldn't do this. Julia, please! Sit down and let me talk to you. You're not making any sense!"

Julia turned around from the windows and ran into her grandmother. She wiggled around her and aimed towards the back of the house again, not hearing anything Mrs. Thurston was saying. "Don't you have someplace to go, Grandmother? I mean. . ." she closed her eyes. *What day was it? Where does grandmother go on what is it, Thursday?* She opened her eyes then. "Your hair. Don't you get your hair done on Thursdays?" It's Thursday. "Surely you need to go so you're ready for the Benefit on Saturday!" Julia took Mrs. Thurston by the arms and ushered her towards the back door picking up purse and keys along the way.

"Julia this is ridiculous! You can't just march into my home and push me out the back door!"

"But you'll be late! Look! It's already half way through the afternoon. Go on. Get your hair done and have tea with somebody important or something. I'll just stay here and watch the house for you."

"I don't need anyone to watch my house, Julia! This has been my home for forty years and it'll go on being my home for forty more. My safe, *unwatched* home!"

"Grandmother, please! Just go!" Julia pleaded with her eyes, her whole body.

Mrs. Thurston looked at her, measured her and then she did the unthinkable. She reached out and pulled Julia into her arms and pressed her head into her shoulder and held her tight. "I don't know what's gotten into you, but I'm glad you came here, to me." She squeezed Julia one extra second before leaning back away from her.

Julia looked into her grandmother's eyes expecting to be reprimanded like the gazillion times before. But to her surprise, her grandmother met her eye to eye. "You take my house and do whatever it is you think you need to do. I'll be back at six. If you're still here we'll have dinner and talk. We have so much to talk about."

Julia sniffed. She nodded.

Mrs. Thurston pressed her with her eyes. "Promise me you won't do anything without thinking it through."

Julia sniffed again and nodded like she had so many times before.

Mrs. Thurston turned and opened the door to leave, but she stilled and looked back at her granddaughter with unfamiliar tenderness. "And Julia?" Her head tilted to the side. "Whatever this is with Bear, look at every side, every possible angle.

It's all I've got to offer you in advice on anything.
I've too often looked at life around me through one
tiny view. It didn't serve me well, either. I've
learned in my old age that there's a lot more to life
than one perspective."

Julia was shocked again that day. Tears ran
down her face, but she nodded. "I'll try."

Her grandmother waited a little too long, there
in that doorway, then turned and left her
granddaughter alone. Julia watched her elder as she
backed out of the garage in her Lincoln Continental.
Mr. Joe waved Mrs. Thurston off on a good
journey. Julia took in the fact that his eyes landed
on her own car in disarray across the back yard.

The question now was, would he be quiet about
her presence? And if so, for how long?

BEAR DROVE STRAIGHT to the mountain,
checked in at Julia's, then Jon and Christy's. Hell,
he even checked in with the *tyrant* of Skyline,
Dicker. Nothing. No one had seen hide nor hair of
his woman anywhere. He'd texted her and got
nothing. He'd called and it had gone straight to
voicemail. She'd turned her phone off and locked
him out. Of course he didn't deserve any better, but

God how he wanted to make sure she was safe. She'd driven away like the fires of hell were after her and he was the cause of her despair. Idiot! Now he sat on the side of a mountain road, idling, thinking, and trying to figure out what to do and where to go next. What a jackass he was! He'd been thinking it was just fine to go on with her, not telling her of his success and his reality. *It wasn't a big deal,* he'd told himself. *She wouldn't care one way or the other*, he'd said. All the while his mother's voice and his sisters, all five of them, voiced their disapproval inside his head. But no, he had to go and be the biggest jerk in the country and keep his personal information to himself. And now the details of her brother's death. What an insensitive fool he'd been. He'd asked her to open up and be honest with him but he hadn't valued her enough to reciprocate.

He slammed the palm of his hand down on the steering wheel and roared an expletive at the world about him. "Where are you, Julia? Where would you go to lick your wounds?" He took in a deep breath and leaned his head back on the headrest to think. If it were him, he'd go straight to family. If not Mama Paula, then one of his sisters, a cousin, an aunt or uncle. But the only family Julia had now was her grandmother. He didn't know if Julia knew what had been discovered, if the two had spoken since he had given his information to Mrs.

Thurston. But regardless, they *were* family, Julia and Mrs. Thurston. Blood *was* something. He let that idea simmer while he checked in with Angel. She hadn't heard from Julia either, so Bear, with nowhere else to go, leapt on the thought and closed the distance.

MR. JOE SAT on the porch of his house, swinging slowly back and forth on the porch swing when Bear pulled up. Bear quietly got out of the car and looked to Mr. Joe for direction. Sure enough, Mr. Joe pointed eyes and hand firmly in the direction of one Mrs. Thurston's house and Bear knew beyond a doubt that he would find his woman there. He didn't bother with the front door. Clearly she'd thought to hide her car, so he took the driveway back at double time and caught her in his arms as she catapulted down the back porch steps. "Princess, please stop and listen to me."

Julia pushed at him, tears flowing freely. Her face was blotched in four shades of red. "You can follow me all you want to, but," she sniffed and wiped at her nose, "I am *not* your princess, *you big*" sniff, *"bear!"* She stomped on his foot like a child for emphasis.

Bear didn't feel a thing. He sighed and, holding her in place, put his head to hers, his mouth in front of hers. "I'm sorry, Julia. I should've told you everything." He nudged her with his nose. She butted him with her head. "Aww, now don't do that, sugar. Please just settle down and talk to me. Let me explain."

"The last time I let a man explain to me why he'd lied, I lost all my money, all my worth." She punched him with both fists in the chest. "You knew that! You knew trusting you wasn't an easy thing for me."

Bear closed his eyes, feeling all the hurt and anger she thrust at him.

"But you did this anyway. You willingly lied to me." Bear's head shot up in disagreement. Julia tried again to pull from his grasp. "Maybe you didn't tell me a lie exactly, but you withheld information that you knew would make a difference to me. Not that the information mattered, but telling me mattered. You hurt me, Bear. You said you would never hurt me for the world." Determined to get free, she wrangled at him. "Remember that? Those were your own words. And here I am again. The stupid, gullible, naive girl who believed another liar."

Bear felt her give up and go still, all the steam leaked out leaving her with no fight left to fuel her emotions. He was encouraged by that, but he felt trouble just the same. He hadn't lived with women for this long not to recognize the imminent storm left to come.

"You know what hurts the most?"

Julia's voice sounded like a whisper, a soft faraway, untouchable whisper that would haunt him for a long time to come if he didn't get this right. "No. Tell me, Princess. Tell me what hurts the worst so I can fix it." He sought her eyes and pulled for her to tell him. Then he let her hands go free and trusted her to further speak his errors for all the world to hear. He wanted her to rail at him, fight him. Just don't be quiet.

As quiet as a little girl, Julia opened up to him. "I did the same thing to you that was done to me my whole life. I discounted you. I made you out to be a failure of a human being for not living up to what I thought you should be." She looked up at him then with fear and sadness filling her face.

Bear wasn't expecting that. He'd hoped for roaring and kicking and slapping and fighting. He could take that. But this. That he had made her cross the line of her own boundaries. That he made her afraid of losing him, too. He'd taken her value and twisted it. Her worth and tarnished it. Unintentional yes, but still, he'd taken something that was spotless and fed her fear of losing something wonderful. He'd risked breaking her heart. Bear reached his hand up to cup her cheek. "I am a loser, Julia. I'm a bum that had the good fortune of being loved and cared for and falling into a skillset that's been good to me. But I am an idiot and a jackass for not telling you everything."

"You're right. You never had to work like me. Your family loved you and cared for you when mine made sure I knew they were displeased with me at every turn. Even in my profession I had to fight to get past that displeasure and failure. But you never had to work past that. And your natural skills shine because of that love and nurturing." She crossed her arms over her heart and held herself tightly. She looked over at Mr. Joe's yard. "I guess Mr. Joe called you, huh?" She laughed sadly at herself and shook her head. "I wondered how much time I had before he did." She looked at Bear then, saw him questioning her. "He waved at grandmother as she drove away. He knew that was my car." She pointed at it.

Bear wasn't quite sure how she managed to get it in at that particular angle. He raised an eyebrow at her over it.

She smiled slightly, then frowned. "I saw your work at the market." She closed her eyes and groaned. "I see now how every time you disappeared you were going to work, not slinking off to ride your bike. You were riding in to town to work in the solitude of your studio." She nodded as if comprehending more of the picture. "I guess that was your dad's storefront when he was alive?"

Bear nodded.

Julia smiled. "I guess that's the place you feel your family support the best. At least that makes sense to me that you would want to be in a familiar comfortable place to paint." She paused, hesitated, really. "You have such spectacular views of life and family, Bear. Beautiful views, really."

Bear slumped inside. He felt like he was losing her. She hadn't seen his vision of her, him, their family. Surely she had seen the painting, you couldn't miss it. But she hadn't recognized herself in its lines and brilliant colors.

"Everything all right here?" Mr. Joe peeked around the corner of the house.

Bear turned and acknowledged the man. "Yes, sir. We're good." He smiled, but worry overshadowed it. "We just need to patch things up a bit."

Mr. Joe, reassured he wouldn't sneak up on anyone unawares, came around the corner and let the tenderness of his years play across his face. "Well now, there's not a one of us ever lived yet that didn't need to patch a thing or two up now and again." He reached over and placed his worn paper-thin-skinned hand on Julia's forearm. "And I can't imagine one any better than this one to patch things up with." He patted her arm gently. "She's one of the good ones, Miss Julia. Always has a smile and a tender word for the world, good or bad." He looked to Bear, face to face, man to man. "You take good care of her, you hear, son? You'll never go wrong with this one. She's a real work of art, this one." He winked, affirming to Bear that he was on to his secrets.

Bear let his chin dip and acknowledged Mr. Joe's words.

Mr. Joe patted Julia one last time before turning to walk away.

"Mr. Joe?" Julia stepped around Bear and put herself directly in front of Mr. Joe. She looked up into his face sniffled and offered up a pitiful smile.

Mr. Joe reached down and pulled her tight for a hug like a father would give his girl. "You go on now, sugar. Patch things up with Bear and make some babies for your grandmother." He wiggled his forehead mischievously. "I think she's finally found her better side."

Bear slapped him on the shoulder as men do and cackled into the wind. "Well, you old dog you! It's about time!" He laughed out loud again.

Julia clearly didn't get it by the way she looked at them puzzled.

"So, does this mean you have a date for the Benefit Saturday night?" Bear prodded.

Mr. Joe split a grin and winked. "Yes siree. I believe it means that and a whole lot more, son!"

161

Julia tracked between them. When she got it, her face lit up like Christmas. "You mean, wait. You and Grandmother?"

Mr. Joe was the one laughing then. "Hells bells, I ain't been watching her house all these years for nothing!"

CHAPTER THIRTEEN

JULIA WATCHED Mr. Joe trail down the old ribbon driveway before turning back to face Bear. He was bigger than life standing there in front of her with his heart outstretched and love filling up the space between them. She was mad at him. Hurt, too. But she had to admit, wrong or not, he was her heart.

Bear stretched his hands out to the side. "Well?"
Julia let her head fall to her shoulder, uncertain what to say. "Well what?"

"It's your call, Princess. Where do we go from here?"

She looked at his hands drop back to his sides. They were such big hands. Strong hands. He was big and strong, too, just like a real bear. But he was kind and loving. He was steady and faithful. Sure. True. He was full of all things good.

Bear quirked an eyebrow at her. "Do you need me to leave you alone to think this through?"

Julia chewed on her lip. He was just a big teddy bear. He meant no harm, she was certain. And all that Mr. Joe had just spoken about her went just as well for Bear. Her Bear. He was a good one. A real work of art.

Julia let her smile shine out into the autumnal daylight and walked right into his arms, slipped her hands around him and said, "I know exactly where we go from here." Mischief beamed from her.

Bear caught on to her. "Yeah? Where's that?"

"The market."

"Now why on earth would you want to go back to the market?" He grinned broadly.

"Well, see?" Julia ducked her head shyly, garnered her courage and looked back to him. "I've wanted to meet *Giocco* for a while now. He's so mysterious and all. And now that I know he's you, well…"

Bear grunted then zeroed in on her with ferocity. "Exactly what did you want from *Giocco*, Julia?"

She snickered. "Well?" She played with a curl in his beard. "Maybe a private show?" Her eyes found his.

Bear's voice went flat. "You want to see my paintings. Alone."

Julia buried her head in his neck and whispered in his ear. "Maybe I want to see more than your paintings."

Bear growled and pushed her up to the porch, forcing her to walk backwards up two steps at eye level to him. She laughed nervously, but then he did the most amazing thing to her. He reached behind her neck with both hands and pulled her close. Touching her nose to his own, he said, "Julia, there is nothing I could ever paint that is as beautiful as you are to me right now. Right here." His eyes searched her face. His fingers soothed her skin. "*la mia Principessa*", he whispered at the sight of her lovely mouth. His eyes searched for hers, hungry for the sight of her. "I will love you always." He opened his lips around hers then and she devoured his words of love.

Julia felt the woman inside her soul flutter and break free at his declaration of love. It was as if she'd waited her whole life for him and he was finally there, right where she needed him most. She pulled away to breathe and looked deep into his eyes. "I think I've waited for you my whole life." She smoothed a wayward strand of hair out of his eyes. "Take me and show me your world of art, please. Like really fast so I can take you home with me. I want to take you home with me, Bear."

Bear sighed showing his relief. "I'm happy to show you anything and everything you want to see at the market." He pointed his head in the direction of her car. "You think you can back out of that predicament over there?"

Julia frowned. "I'm not sure." She laughed under her breath. "It seemed a good place when I pulled into the yard." A few bricks trailed the back left tire from where she'd dislodged them from the flower bed she'd obviously driven over when she'd pulled into the yard.

"I don't think you were seeing anything very well when you pulled in here, sugar."

Julia laid her head to hide on Bear's shoulder. "I won't apologize. I was hurt and distraught. I needed a safe place to think."

"To hide, you mean." Bear grumbled.

Julia nodded into his shoulder. "I guess I did need to hide. I needed time to sort it all out."

Bear nudged her head. "Come on. You got it in there, you can get it out. Then follow me to the market." He pushed her away then so she could see his face. "I need you, Julia. I need to show you everything. But. . ."

Fear threatened Julia's mind. "But?"

"But you're going to have to come back here afterwards." Bear groaned aloud. "Not that that's what I want, mind you. But it's what has to be."

Still concerned, Julia dared ask, "But why?"

"I can't tell you this one. Your grandmother needs to tell you. But it needs to happen today."

"You're scaring me. Grandmother never needs to talk to me." She worried her lip again. "Come to think of it, she said something about needing to talk if I was here when she got back." She shook off the worry that pushed at her. "But there's not a thing in the world she and I have to talk about. Right?" She questioned Bear.

Bear ran a hand through his hair, the way he always did when he got cornered. "I can't tell you what she needs to talk about. But I can tell you what it's not." He smiled broadly.

"You look up to no good. Spill." She pinched him in the side, goading him to tell his secrets.

"Well, I know she and Mr. Joe aren't getting married because she's pregnant!" And he chuckled with laughter all the way to her car, backing it out of the precarious position she'd left it in, while she looked on, loving him even more.

TRUE TO HIS word, Bear met Julia at the market and showcased what remained in his studio since most was already hung at the reception hall in preparation for the weekend. In the process, he gave her a tour of the old building, accentuating it with memories of his childhood and filling in more of his background. To redeem himself from being too secret, she supposed.

It was amazing to hear of his family life as a child. How his parents acknowledged his artistic talent at a young age and, sacrificing their own time with him, placed him at the feet of a master painter in Bologna, Italy. He had spent every summer break, from sixth grade on studying and growing his craft with various teachers in and around Bologna, living with Mama Paula's family who still maintained the Raimondo Family Farm just outside of the city. They were so much a part of his life that he continued his stay and attended the University of Bologna after finishing high school. Now he maximized that learning each and every day painting Italian landscapes. He still took in house painting jobs on occasion. It started out as a way to make extra money when he was younger, but ended up being his cover story to maintain his anonymity. That job would end after this weekend, he'd assured her. Every now and again he could also be found teaching a painting class or two, here or abroad. He didn't much care where he found himself so long as he had his paints and his bike. But he always came home. Family was his center. The paint and the biking were what made the rest of life fun. But now he hoped Julia would help him build a home. A place to call his own. A point to grow from. Together with her.

It didn't surprise her to find his minimalistic ways when he took her upstairs to his living quarters inside the old store room. It held only a bed, a microwave, a dorm sized refrigerator and a bathroom in the back corner. A window overlooked the alleyway on one end, another over the street side. An extender hook on the back of the door held his entire wardrobe beyond the paint clothes he kept in his beater truck. Abashedly, he'd admitted, bike clothes didn't need to be hung, just washed and worn.

After spending several hours reminding her of his passion for her body, Bear gave her the most beautiful thing anyone had ever presented her with, his dream of the future. The painting of Skyline. Of her. Their home.

ON FRIDAY EVENING, Julia found herself alone, lounging in a bathtub full of relaxation. Bear had been summoned by his entourage of sisters for a night of cleaning. His cleaning, Julia suspected.

A candle flickered nearby and she let its glow soothe her. She recalled the previous day's discoveries and let them wash over her as she played with the bubbles in her bath. Saturday morning would be full of manicures and pedicures and having her hair done. But for tonight, fully satiated in new love, Julia simply relaxed and dreamed of her man before heading off to bed.

Bear told her he wouldn't see her again until he picked her up the next night. He had to go with Nicki on Saturday morning to make sure all was set at the reception hall. And it being Nicki, everything would take much longer to set up to her perfect standards and then reset again because she was fickle that way.

Julia smiled at the way he mimicked his sister. He wasn't fond of the idea, but he was willing to cooperate with Nicki because she was family, bossy as she was. And because she had done nothing but given him her complete support his whole life. With the exception of that time in Milan with their cousin Andre, of course.

The idea of family brought her mind around to the early evening meal she'd shared with her grandmother. Nothing could have shocked her more than things Mrs. Thurston disclosed to her. Julia's brother Lance was gone. Such a sad and painful thing to learn. Somewhere deep in her heart she'd always imagined him coming back, making amends, changing the way he'd left her and making it right. But that wasn't going to happen. She turned her head and looked at the photo of him laughing with her in their youth. Mrs. Thurston had insisted she keep it, along with the other things that had belonged to Lance. Maybe someday Julia would be able to read the letters and sentiments he left behind. For now, she'd taken his photo and placed it inside of the bottom edge of her bathroom mirror to help her remember the good times she had shared with him. Soon she would find a frame for it. But for now, it was close at hand and a reminder of how precious life was. It's value undefinable.

Looking at the photo now, in the quiet of the evening, she allowed herself the opportunity to recall the time it had been taken. It was in the summer before Julia had gone to middle school and would be separated away from Lance. Leaving him behind in elementary school, she remembered, was a little scary and somewhat exciting. Being the older of the two had always been like that, exciting and scary at the same time.

It was also the year her family had gone to the beach, Gulf Shores if she remembered correctly. They had rented a brightly painted cottage right near the water's edge. It was a small house, with only two bedrooms. And it was a funny house what with its stilts, or *legs* as she had called them, sticking deep into the ground for a foundation which in turn raised the house high up into the air. The best part of the cottage was its steps that led directly to the sandy beach. There were no streets to cross or pathways to follow. It was simply there. The whole ocean docked at its feet.

She and Lance had shared a room together that was furnished with a bunk bed. It too had been painted in bright colors with fun and fanciful seahorses accentuating its frame. She smiled at remembering Lance's excitement over having to climb a ladder to reach his bed at night. It had been a thrill for him. The same seahorse design had been carried over into the bathroom furnishings. She had loved that little cottage by the sea.

The days at the beach were full of sunshine, laughter, and soft ocean breezes coming in off of the water. Bike riding had been as frequent as outings into the ocean water. The evenings were spectacular with the sun dripping each night below the horizon. Nothing in the world was as beautiful as that orange ball slipping underneath the water in its grand and magical display of closing out the day. The sounds of surf had lulled her to sleep each night. And though they rarely found many unbroken seashells, they woke up each and every morning to go hunting for what the tides had left behind in their wake.

For her parents, the days had been full of lounging in the sun, watching Julia and Lance chase after the seagulls and laughing when they reached up to feed the large birds who dipped into the wind to catch their offerings. She remembered her father had rented a boat to take out into the gulf one day. He had wanted to feel the wind in his face, he'd said. And he'd piled them all up into the boat and taken them for the ride of their lives. Her mother had looked like a movie star with her big, dark sunglasses on her face and her hair whipping around behind her in the wind. Her father had been in command of his ship that day and proud to be the man he was.

She remembered the shock at feeling all that water underneath them. For some reason she had expected it to be smooth and soft, but it was rough and harsh and a little bit frightening. But it did give her something of a private feeling, having all that wind and noise around her to drown out the world. That had been a strange and wonderful thing, to feel isolated and alone yet surrounded by everyone she held dear to her heart. It had been like a silent movie. She could see them all around her, relishing the awe and grandeur of the place and time, but the familiar sounds of their voices and laughter were eaten up by the roar of the boat's engine and the winds and the water.

Before their return to land is when the photo had been taken. She laughed out loud at the memory the picture gave her and wondered why she had not remembered that precise frame of time since it had happened. It had been such a warm and happy incident in her life, that moment.

While they had been out in the boat, her father had anchored the vessel for a little while to give them all an opportunity to hear the silence of the wind and feel the water rocking underneath them without the engine's power and roar. He'd handed out fishing poles to each of them and let them try to catch a fish. She and her mother had given up quickly, but Lance was certain if he stood there long enough he'd get a bite. And he had. He'd caught a large fish of some type, she couldn't remember what kind it was. But then Lance had felt bad for the fish and had wanted to let it go free. He wanted it to be with the other fishes in the sea. And so her dad had let it go.

Just after letting the fish go free is when the photo had been taken. Lance had snuggled up as close to Julia as their life vests would allow and said something silly about the fish needing to be with his big sister and they had giggled together about it. And just at the time when they were laughing their mother had snapped the photo. They were all so very happy in that moment, all of them laughing together, not a care in the world. It had been a beautiful moment, frozen in time.

Julia let the memory wash over her and she smiled. That's how she would choose to remember her brother. That day on the boat, when his heart was wide open and full of love and they were all together with her parents. That is how she would remember him. Her wonderful brother, unharmed by the harsh realities of the years that followed.

Her bath water grew cold and Julia resigned herself to dry off and get ready for a night of sleep. But tonight she would sleep better, knowing in her heart that there had been better times. They had been real, those happy times. And she had finally made peace with the memories of her brother and lay the past, for all its unfortunate ups and downs, to rest.

Before curling into the softness of her bed, she checked her phone for any missed messages. One from her bestie read simply,

One more night until we have some grown up fun!

Julia typed a quick response, reminding Christy she'd pick her up the next morning at nine sharp and said good night.

The other message was from Bear.

I love you, Princess. Sleep well. Tomorrow I will find you.

Julia pulled the phone close to her heart and fell asleep holding it there and dreamed of a bear dancing with a princess under the stars of a moonlit night.

CHAPTER FOURTEEN

EVERYTHING WAS IN place. Champagne, glasses, flowers. All set inside the limousine. Music played softly as the car came to a stop. Bear breathed in, committed to make this happen. The door opened as the driver attended his duties. Bear nodded to himself, then to the driver, and proceeded to unfold himself out of the car.

"Mr. Grecco," the man bowed and made a grand gesture, "the night is yours." He encouraged Bear, then relaxed into familiarity. "Your lady could not want for a better man than you, my friend."

Bear slapped him on the shoulder good naturedly. "Your old man was kind to let you do this for me tonight, Matt."

Matt nodded. "Dad was glad to have the help what with all the fine folks of Riverland calling on him to transport them to this shindig." He laughed then, humored by the whole affair. "It's not often we get the big celebrities in this town, either. You *know* he's making a killing tonight, what with pulling in a fee from the car services he arranged out of Huntsville and Nashville, too."

Bear laughed with him and nodded his agreement. "He's a good businessman, your dad. I heard someone came in from New York City and another from Milan to bid on the painting."

Matt whistled. "What a night!"

Bear aimed his eyes back towards Julia's front door. "Doesn't matter much to me, though. I only have one painting on my mind."

Matt turned serious. "You've got everything you need, right?"

Bear reached his hand into the right pocket of his jacket to assure himself of its contents. "I think so." He smiled broadly. "Just keep everything ready. I'll be back in a few."

Bear rang the doorbell and waited what seemed like an eternity. And when the door opened, the most beautiful woman he'd ever seen stood before him, arrayed in magically spun silk and light.

Her eyes were soft like morning dew, looking up at him in a smidgeon of uncertainty. "Oh Bear!" she exclaimed. "Your beard." She searched his eyes.

177

Bear smiled and gave her a three hundred and sixty degree turn of himself.

"And your hair." She reached out and ran her hand along his jaw, feeling the closely trimmed beard against her palm before slipping it back into his hair.

"I knew the divas would make me clean up my appearance." Bear's eyes sparkled at her. "I hoped you would like it." He reached out and touched her face with his thumb. Sweeping it across her cheeks he leaned down and kissed her lips and whispered to her, "*tu sei la mia Principessa.*"

Julia laid a hand against his lapel. Holding him at a short distance, she questioned him softly. "What did you say to me?"

Bear pulled back, tilted his head. "You are my princess." He searched her eyes watching and waiting for her confirmation. And nothing was more exhilarating than the smile that spread across her features, assuring him that the night's events would unfold in his favor.

UPON ARRIVING AT the Benefit for the Children's Center for the Arts, Bear and Julia were joined by Jon and Christy, Mama Paula and his five diva sisters. Counting all of them and their dates, with Mr. Joe and Mrs. Thurston thrown in for good measure, they took up the space of several tables near the front of the hall. Photographers flashed on and off again. The news media was not letting this event go unnoticed. Bear looked to be unfazed by the whole affair.

Looking around the room, Julia noted the royalty of Riverland, Alabama. Lurain Rivers, internationally known as the award winning children's author L.V. Kipling, sat to the far side of the room. Ms. Rivers' family surrounded her, including her granddaughter Rina Pearl, the equally award winning blues musician. Julia had been told they would be there. She had been a fan of L.V. Kipling's since she was a child and could not believe her good fortune to be in the same room with such a celebrity. Julia owned every one of Ms. Kipling's books and utilized them to help her students develop a love for reading.

Near the middle of the room was a table fully occupied by people dressed in the kind of flair known only in the great halls of runway models. Each of them wore generous smiles and stunning beauty in the way Julia had grown to expect of Bear's family. It was Mama Paula's relatives, mixing themselves in with the American side of the family, celebrating the success of *Giocco*, their very own Giovani Columbera Grecco.

A hand reached around Julia, offering her a glass of sparkling bubbles. Bear slipped his head down and around her neck, kissing tenderly underneath the velvet of her ear. "I love you, Princess." The words were so new, Julia basked in them and let her eyes dip in the wonder of his love. She turned to face him and looked up to see the beauty his sisters had uncovered. He was magnificent. He was sculpted in masculinity and finesse like no other. "I love you too, Bear." She smiled.

Bear rocked back a little ways. "That's the first time you've said those words to me, you know."

She dipped her head, ran a finger around the rim of her champagne glass and nodded before looking back up. "I know. I didn't want to say them until I was certain." She shrugged bashfully.

"And now you're sure?" Worry skittered across Bear's face before he could hide it.

Julia quickly bobbed her head up and down. "I'm absolutely positive."

Bear relaxed himself. "Then let's make our first toast." He tipped his glass to touch hers. "To you. To us. To love."

"Yes. To Love. Our love."

Bear took her glass then and set it aside. He pulled her close. "Come with me outside for a minute, will you? I have something for you." He smiled, his eyes dancing in their excitement. "I planned to give it to you at the end of the evening, but I can't wait another minute."

Julia was puzzled. "You have something for me? A gift?" She laughed out loud at him, enamored by his generosity. "You're going to spoil me, you know."

He agreed. "Yes, and it will be my pleasure, too! But this gift is different. And I admit, I'm being very selfish giving it to you now, so early in the evening."

"Selfish? Why is that?"

"Because I want you to be able to show it off all evening long. I want everyone to see my gift to you, even the press from around the world."

His tenderness melted her heart. "Well then, let me have it so I can show the world how wonderful you are to me." She giggled, much like the bubbles in the champagne.

And with that, he pulled her outside, stopping only when he reached the fountain in the garden outside of the event hall. And in what seemed a magical fairytale, like that of her dreams in the night before, Bear knelt on one knee, bowed in her honor, and presented her with a velvet box.

Julia gasped in shock. She didn't in her wildest dreams expect this tonight, *his* night of glory.

He looked up into her eyes, his whole heart there between them. "You are my Princess, Julia. You are my world. Please do me the honor of becoming my Queen?" He lifted the lid of the box and shining out at her was a beautifully and delicately designed version of the masculine crown he wore upon his wrist and signed upon each of his master works.

Julia covered her shock with her hands. Never in her wildest dreams could she be loved more wonderfully than by her Bear. She was speechless. Her heart was so full. Tears filled her eyes and all she could do was nod.

"Is that a yes?"

Julia nodded more vigorously and Bear stood and lifted her high up into his arms triumphantly. Julia wrapped her hands around his neck and sliding down, she reached his lips and let him feel her love for him.

Bear pulled away and let out a shout of celebration and pumped his arm in the air, crowing in delight of her acceptance. Then he reached down and tenderly placed the ring on her finger. "I promise to always love you, Julia. My Princess. My soon to be Queen."

Drama of every kind erupted because of the night's revelations. Riverland's own Bear Grecco was the renowned *Giocco*, the artist taking the world by a storm. That's what the news headlines said the following day. And sorry ladies, but he's taken. By a princess, no less.

Rina Pearl won the highest bid of the night and welcomed *Giocco's* painting, entitled *Raimondo Farm Road,* into her personal collection. The Children's Center for the Arts received far more funds than expected. They had more than enough necessary to build, furnish, and stock their new facility with the makings of a scholarship fund as well. *Giocco's* painting brought in a whopping seven figures, making it his highest priced painting so far.

Mrs. Thurston had agreed to dance with Mr. Joe that night, in front of all the world to see. Because well, she could let herself celebrate in the limelight together with her granddaughter. Dicker was on his best behavior for a change, tapping his feet to the music, dancing with anyone who would allow him near. Mama Paula was not in that particular mix of women.

But the night offered other announcements worthy of celebration. Bear proudly presented his fiancé to every person who came near him and Julia. Christy was ecstatic at Julia's request that Christy stand by her for the wedding. In fact, Julia wanted both Christy and Rudi to be in the middle of the wedding events, as well as the other one Christy kept eating cookies and sweets for, she teased. Yes, there was a brand new baby on its way to the Fraser family, due to arrive by springtime.

But that's not the end of this story. Because come spring?

Well . . . you'll see.

*Just in time for Valentine's Day
an anthology chock full of*

MISTAKEN IDENTITIES
Past. Present. Future.

by
Bambi Lynn
Lesia Flynn
Amy Boyles

*Skyline Mountain is in the mix with Ben and
the love of his life, Cassidy.*

REMEMBERING SKYLINE
eBook Only!

You won't want to miss this crazy fun story!

*Available
February 3, 2015!*

REMEMBERING SKYLINE
Skyline Mountain Book 3

BEN HAS BEEN hanging Christmas lights during his down season for years. It was simply what he did to get by from one river cabin season to the next. But this year, due to an unfortunate incident, he finds himself in the emergency room. When he walks out of the hospital, having no memory of his life before, he assumes the role of a Scotsman figuring that's who he is since there's a kilt hanging in his closet, fresh from the dry cleaners. The only thing is, he's not Scottish at all. But he can't be talked out if it and assumes the randy role with gusto.

CASSIDY HAS HAD enough! And Ben is at the top of her list. She's been trying for years to get Ben's attention. But no. Not until he's lost all of his memory, that is. Now she can't get away from him and he doesn't even know his own name.

If you enjoyed reading Painting Skyline,
I would be grateful if you would help others
enjoy this book, too.

Recommend it. Please help other readers
discover this book by recommending it to friends,
reader groups, book clubs, and discussion boards.

Review it. Please tell other readers why you
liked this book by reviewing it on Amazon or
Goodreads. And if you do review it, please contact
me so I can thank you with a personal note or visit
me at http://www.LesiaFlynn.com.

*Lesia Flynn's Newsletter
is coming your way very soon!*

You don't want to miss it!
Watch for details at Lesia Flynn's
various social media platforms so you too
can receive regular updates and participate
in giveaways and fun!

ABOUT THE AUTHOR

Lesia Flynn is a native of Louisiana. She studied graphic design at LA Tech University. She lives in northern Alabama with her husband, children, and a rescue cat named Chali2Na who is determined to save her from her daily goofball mishaps. She enjoys reading, writing, music and art, but most of all, anything that provides an adventure! Lesia loves hearing from fans.

Connect with Lesia Flynn online:

www.LesiaFlynn.com
facebook.com/pages/Lesia-Flynn
Twitter: @LesiaFlynn
Pinterest: Lesia Flynn

Made in the USA
Charleston, SC
28 May 2015